RON ORLIS
AND THE
MYSTERIOUS
INTRUDER

RON ORLIS

AND THE

MYSTERIOUS INTRUDER

BERNARD PALMER

Please note that several books in the Danny Orlis series are published by Sword of the Lord Publications and are available for purchase on their website, www.swordbooks.com.

Aneko Press *Youth*

www.anekopress.com

Aneko Press, Life Sentence Publishing, and our logos are trademarks of Life Sentence Publishing, Inc.
203 E. Birch Street
P.O. Box 652
Abbotsford, WI 54405

JUVENILE FICTION / Religious / Christian / Action & Adventure

Paperback ISBN: 979-8-88936-092-6

eBook ISBN: 979-8-88936-093-3

10 9 8 7 6 5 4 3 2 1

Available where books are sold

CONTENTS

Ch. 1: A Strange Welcome 1

Ch. 2: The Trouble Begins 11

Ch. 3: More Opposition 21

Ch. 4: Detective Work 33

Ch. 5: Friends in Need... 43

Ch. 6: A Favor Repaid.. 53

Ch. 7: A Well-Arranged Accident.. 63

Ch. 8: Strong Medicine.. 71

Ch. 9: Wet Rescue 87

Ch. 10: A Theft 97

Ch. 11: True Confession.. 107

CHAPTER 1

A STRANGE WELCOME

Doug Davis walked away from his triplet brother, Del, and moved quietly to the far end of the dock. For some minutes, he continued to squint at the distant reaches of the great lake, ignoring the hushed murmur of waves on the beach. The boat he and Del had been watching since it left the mission pier was lost in the shimmering sheen of sun and water, its existence betrayed only by the throaty growl of the powerful outboard that was fading into the distance.

At last, he turned to his brother, his dark eyes curious. "Why do you suppose he came over here, anyway?" he asked. "He didn't want to borrow anything, and he sure didn't come to visit."

Del nodded but remained silent a few more moments. Doug was right about the man who had just left. The man had said he was Dr. Mulligan and had asked what was going on at Ron Orlis's mission station. Doug had explained that they had intended to help Ron build two more rooms onto their tiny house. The formidable-looking man went on to explain that he was an anthropologist and that he did not appreciate Ron Orlis's trying to "Americanize" the Indians there in northern Canada. Dr. Mulligan made no effort to mask his dislike of them.

"I think," Del finally answered, "he wanted to scare us away."

The boys left the dock and made their way past the brightly hued fishing boats that were pulled up on shore. An Indian boy about their age approached. Their eyes met his, solemnly. They would have spoken, but there was no sign of friendliness or welcome in his gaze – only hostility. It was as though he sensed they wanted to be friendly and was shutting it off before it started.

Another time, Doug would have been disturbed enough to take note of the boy's hostility, but at the moment, he could think only of their American visitor.

"What difference would it make to Dr. Mulligan whether Ron and Darlene stay here or not? He doesn't live up here. He isn't even an Indian. I can't believe he really cares that much about anybody."

"I know, but he's sure uptight about something." They stopped and leaned against one of the cumbersome, flat-bottomed boats that lined the pier at the end of the day.

"He doesn't like the idea of you and me being here this summer, I know," Doug said.

"I can't figure that out, either," Del said. "We aren't going to cause him any trouble."

"That isn't what worries me. I hope he doesn't cause *us* any trouble."

Del laughed at him. "You're something else! You've always got to have something to worry about, don't you?"

"OK. OK. Forget I said anything." Doug laughed too.

Neither of the boys mentioned the American stranger again until they were at the dinner table that evening. "Ron," Doug began, "does Dr. Mulligan come over here to see you very often?"

"Nope." Ron Orlis did not look up. "This was the first time."

"Why do you suppose he came?"

Ron shook his head. "Don't know, unless he's afraid I've called in reinforcements."

Ron's wife, Darlene, glanced at her two little boys at the table between herself and her husband and shivered. "There's something odd about that man." She shivered again.

Ron scolded her mildly. "You shouldn't say that. Dr. Mulligan's alright when you get acquainted with him."

"You know what I mean," she persisted. "It isn't that I dislike him personally. I'm sure he's a nice individual, but I don't like his opposition to our work. He acts as though we're criminals or something."

"You can't let that bother you, Darlene. He's got some odd ideas as to our reasons for being here."

"Like what?"

"I've talked with him a few times," Ron explained. "He thinks we're here to convince the people they should give up their old culture and become like white men. That's the reason he's so opposed to our being here on the reserve and building an addition to our house and establishing ourselves permanently."

"That's not true!" she protested. "I've heard you say a hundred times that you feel the Indian people should maintain their own identity and lifestyle, except for improving their physical condition."

He nodded. "All we're really here to do is to tell them about the Lord Jesus Christ, and what He can do in their lives. They'll make changes on their own after they've accepted Him."

"We know that," Darlene continued, "and I hope the people know we love them too." She looked at Ron seriously. "But he's really getting in with some of the people. He could cause us real trouble. I guess that's the reason I'm so disturbed about his being here."

"Daddy won't let him keep us from telling the people about Jesus," six-year-old Robbie said impulsively. "Will you, Daddy."

"*Jesus* won't let him keep us from telling the people about Him, Robbie," Ron corrected him.

Robbie smiled brightly. "I guess that's what 1 meant."

Shortly after that, the subject was changed, but Doug still could not push aside the fear in Darlene's eyes. She was not the kind to get concerned without cause. When she was upset, there had to be a reason. He was still thinking about it as he went to bed that night.

* * *

Del and Doug had been looking forward to fishing in Canada from the day they first got Ron's invitation to spend the summer helping with the mission building project, but they supposed they would not be able to get out on the lake until the work was well under way. But they had been at Ron's for three days, and they still were not able to start work. The material was not at the building site, and Ron did not know when he would be able to get it there. The lumber was stacked at the sawmill behind Gordon's Trading Post across the lake, where it had been since it was cut and planed the fall before. The cement, chipboard, and paint had also been left at Gordon's by the Cat train that brought supplies north over the ice in the wintertime.

Gordon had agreed to bring it over on his barge, but he had been so busy since breakup that he said he had not been able to get around to it. "I'll have to go over and see him this afternoon," Ron said at the breakfast table.

"Why don't we bring back the cement so we can get the foundation run?" Del suggested. "Then we could be ready to go to work when he gets the lumber over here."

Ron nodded his agreement. "I was thinking it would be alright for you guys to go fishing today, but it would be better to get the foundation run first."

As soon as they finished breakfast, they crossed the lake in the mission boat to the independent trader's store on the opposite side. The lake was big, and even though the waves were small and they were able to run at top speed, it took almost an hour to reach Gordon's dock.

"I sure wouldn't want to be caught out here in a storm," Del observed, looking about.

"If you're ever on this lake and the wind comes up, get to the closest shore and wait for it to go down," Ron warned. "That's the only safe thing to do."

The Davis boys tried to mask their apprehension. Doug did not realize at first why he was so concerned about rough water. He could swim well, and it did not bother him to be out in a boat. It did not seem reasonable that he would be so afraid of being caught on the lake in a storm. Then he remembered. The Davis triplets' parents had lost their lives in a boating accident. The children had been only eleven then, and Doug did not remember much about it.

Even though it had happened years before, he was still disturbed when Ron mentioned that this lake could be dangerous.

Ron turned off the big outboard motor suddenly, and the boat glided to a halt. The boys turned quickly to stare at him. "Why're we stopping out here?" Del wanted to know. They were still a hundred yards from the end of the dock.

"I don't happen to have an extra prop to spare, so I thought we'd better pole through the shallow water."

Several men were sitting on the steps of the trading post when they secured the boat to the dock. A few of them spoke to Ron but the others eyed him sullenly. Doug and Del were surprised at the way Ron was able to ignore their unspoken opposition. He greeted them all warmly and with respect.

The pudgy trader was in the ramshackle building, leaning against the counter when they entered. He greeted Ron defensively. "I told you I wouldn't be able to get your stuff hauled over for a while."

"We came over to get the cement."

Gordon scowled. "You can get it all yourself, if you want to. Haulin' supplies across the lake don't mean that much to me."

"We just came for the cement." Ron acted as though he had not even heard the dislike in the other man's voice. "Please haul the lumber over for me as soon as you can."

Gordon turned his head and spit a stream of

tobacco juice in the direction of the coffee can on the floor near the stove, missing it by half a foot. "I ain't got no help, y'know. I can't just drop everything and run clear across the lake every time somebody whistles. I got to take care of business."

Del and Doug could not see what business he was talking about. There were a number of men on the building steps, but there were no customers inside, and the dust on the shelves spoke mutely of inactivity.

"Have you got the key to the shed where the cement's stored?" Ron asked him.

Gordon jerked his head in the direction of the shed behind the trading post. "It's unlocked."

For the first time, concern clouded the missionary's handsome face. "You said you'd keep it locked."

The trader pulled himself erect and wiped his hands on the broad expanse of shirt that covered his protruding stomach. "You *asked* to leave your stuff out there. I never told you I'd be responsible for it."

Ron was about to retort quickly but changed his mind. His smile returned as his irritation fled. "I was just surprised it was unlocked, that's all."

The trader's manner seemed to change. "It ain't been unlocked too long," he said. "I had to go out for some stuff a couple of weeks ago and forgot to lock it again. But everything's there. You don't have to worry about that."

Ron thanked him and started for the door. Del and Doug were right behind him.

As they approached the shed, Ron quickened his pace. The door was half ajar, sagging wearily on its hinges. The rusted padlock was hanging from the door casing.

"I don't think Mr. Gordon was telling the truth when he said the door's been locked all winter," Doug said, indicating the rust on the padlock.

"Maybe he did get a little carried away, but I still think everything's here," Ron replied.

They pushed the door open and stepped inside, blinking as their eyes grew accustomed to the half-light. Del went over to the pile of cement sacks in the corner.

"You were right about one thing," he said. "The cement's still here, at least."

"I was sure it would be."

Doug caught his breath. "Take a look at this, will you?" He pounded on the top sack. It had been ripped open, and the cement granite hard.

"Ruined!" Dismay edged the missionary's voice. He kicked the other sacks. They were as hard as the first one.

"It must have leaked rain in here," Del said.

But Ron disagreed. "A leaking roof didn't ruin this cement! It was deliberate!"

The boys both gasped in amazement.

"It had to be," Ron continued bleakly. "Every sack has been torn open! Somebody knew this cement belonged to us and ruined it!"

CHAPTER 2

THE TROUBLE BEGINS

There were times when Del and Doug could not understand Ron Orlis. The trader had given his word that he would keep the shed locked, but he had not done it. Now Ron's cement was ruined, and they could not start the building project without it. They both thought he should go to old Gordon about it. This, Ron refused to do.

"Mr. Gordon was just careless. He didn't leave the shed unlocked purposely."

"Maybe he didn't," Del retorted, "but he did let somebody get in here and ruin it. The least he could do is to pay for the cement."

The young missionary disagreed with that. "I think we'd better forget it." He turned and started around the trading post building toward the front door. The boys followed him, still voicing their annoyance.

"You are going to call in the police, aren't you?" Doug asked.

"For six sacks of cement? I think whoever ruined our cement would like it if we did. Half the men on the reserve would be mad at us if we brought in the RCMP for something like this." He stopped and turned deliberately, lowering his voice. "No, we're not going to say anything to anyone about it. We'll go back to the Hudson Bay Store, and radio for another six bags."

Ron went directly to the Hudson Bay Store on their side of the lake and sent a message to the mission pilot, briefly explaining what happened and asking him to bring in the order of cement as soon as he could fit it into his schedule.

When he finished, the Hudson Bay Store manager eyed him quizzically. "You had that cement in Gordon's shed, didn't you?"

Ron nodded.

"How'd it get wet?"

"I really don't know." He changed the subject quickly, but not before the people in the store heard what he had said. A few men sidled closer. Ron did not look at them, but he knew they were curious, waiting for him to continue.

"Do you reckon someone did it purposely?" the Bay manager continued.

"I don't know of anyone who'd do a thing like that."

"I do." The manager snorted. "Right offhand, I

can think of a dozen who would like to cause you trouble. A lot of people on the reserve don't buy that religion of yours."

"How much is the radio message?" Ron asked, pointedly.

The other man realized the missionary would say no more about the incident and allowed the subject to die.

Del and Doug spent the rest of the day fishing. But even though Ron told them exactly where to go, they came in that evening with only three small jacks and a pickerel. The missionary looked at their catch and laughed.

"I'm glad I'm not depending on you guys to catch enough fish to feed me and my family."

"How do you expect us to catch fish on a strange lake if we don't know where to go?" Doug countered.

"I told you everything I know about where to fish."

Del's eyelids squinted against the brilliant afternoon sun. "That's probably the trouble," he said. "When it comes to fishing, you must not know much."

"Don't blame me for your troubles. When I go fishing, I don't miss."

They went in for supper then and were still at the table talking about the fishing trip when there was a knock on the back door. It was an Indian lad two or three years younger than the Davis boys; he was lanky and almost as tall as they were.

Ron greeted him as Stan. "I'd almost forgotten you were coming tonight."

The boy hesitated. "We're going to have our Bible study, aren't we?"

"Sure we are – as soon as we finish eating." He introduced the newcomer to Del and Doug. "They've been giving me a bad time about the fishing here, Stan. They claim there aren't any fish in the lake."

"There are plenty of jacks and pickerel." He spoke seriously. "Even lake trout."

"We didn't say there aren't any fish in the lake," Doug said. "We just claim that Ron doesn't know where to get 'em."

The missionary's laughter filled the kitchen. "I guess I'll have to get you to tell them where to go, Stan."

"I can catch lots of fish for them."

When the Bible study was over an hour later, the Davis boys made arrangements for the young Indian boy to take them out on the lake the next morning.

"I'll meet you down at the boat about seven o'clock," he promised. "OK?"

"Why don't you come and have breakfast with us tomorrow?" Darlene suggested.

Stan winced and looked nervous, as though he feared coming to the missionary's house to eat, but he agreed to come. "I'll be here at six-thirty, then?" There was a question in his voice.

He came to the missionary's home for breakfast shortly before six-thirty the next morning.

Ron went to the door in answer to his knock. "You're early, Stan. Your grandfather must have pulled you out of bed today."

The boy looked frightened. "You won't tell him I came here, will you?"

Ron was surprised at the pleading tone in his voice.

"He'll beat me if he knows."

When they finished eating breakfast, Del and Doug gathered their fishing gear and made their way down to the lake with Stan Ross.

"Is the fishing really as good here as everybody says it is?" Del asked, as they sauntered down the path.

"Oh, it's good, alright," Stan, in the lead, turned and replied.

"But we don't see anybody fishing with lures."

Stan paused. "The white man always goes at things backward. Why should we fish with hooks when we can put out a net and get fish so much easier?"

They were approaching the little log house where Stanley lived with his grandfather. Del and Doug did not know this, so they were surprised when the Indian boy stopped abruptly.

"What's the matter?" Doug asked.

Stan still did not move. "You'd better go ahead. I'll come later." He seemed like he was awfully scared of something and was trying to hide it. He turned and started away.

"Hey," Del exclaimed, "What's this all about? What's wrong?"

Stan went scurrying off in the opposite direction from the lake without looking back. The boys watched until he was out of sight.

"What do you suppose got into him?" Doug asked.

Before Del could answer, the cabin door creaked open, and an elderly Indian appeared. He was a gaunt, wrinkled, little man, bent heavily over his cane. As they watched him, the old Indian took two steps forward, wobbling uncertainly.

"That must be Stan's grandfather!" Doug whispered.

Del nodded. "Do you suppose that's the reason he took off the way he did?"

Anger glittered in the old Indian's watery eyes as he advanced shakily toward them. They felt their cheeks go pale and their hands become moist.

While they stared, held fast by the old man's fury, an all-too-familiar voice was clearly audible behind him.

"That's them!" Dr. Mulligan exclaimed, his voice harsh. "They're staying with that missionary! They've made friends with your grandson, Okimaw. They're going to help Orlis steal Stanley away from you!"

"I warned him to stay away from them!" Okimaw croaked venomously. "I warned him, but he wouldn't listen!"

"You don't need to get so upset," Dr. Mulligan was speaking even louder now. It seemed to the boys that he wanted to be sure they heard him. "All you've got to do is warn these kids. They're smart enough to know they don't want trouble with you! They'll leave Stanley alone!"

Old Okimaw stood motionless, the fire of his dark eyes burning into them. They recoiled self-consciously, taking a step backward.

"You leave him alone!" The old man's voice quavered as it rose. "You leave Stanley alone, if you know what's good for you!"

Dr. Mulligan came up beside Okimaw and put a hand on his shoulder. "They heard you, Okimaw. I don't think you'll have to worry about them anymore."

The old man shook the white man's hand away, contemptuously. For a few more moments, he did not move. Then, abruptly, he turned and hobbled back into the house. Dr. Mulligan followed him and closed the door.

The boys left the little cabin and went down the path to the mission boat on the shore near the government dock. By this time, they were more calm about what had happened.

"I don't think he liked us," Doug said.

"Whatever gave you that idea?"

They put their gear into the boat and sat down on the beach to wait for Stan to return.

"Stan must have seen that his grandfather was watching and was scared to be seen with us; so he skinned out."

"And I can't say that I blame him." Doug shuddered.

"I sure wouldn't want to have to face that old man alone. I can tell you that."

"He's not big enough to hurt us," Del remarked.

"Maybe not." Doug glanced back at the cabin. "But I still wouldn't want to have trouble with him. I've never seen anyone so mad at us."

Del and Doug thought Stanley Ross would be rejoining them shortly, but they waited for half an hour, and there was no sign of him.

"I'm beginning to think he's not coming," Doug said, looking at his watch once more.

"We might as well go fishing without him. I'm sure he's not going to come now, and I can't say that I blame him."

Together, they struggled to push the heavy, flat-bottomed boat into the water. It was all they could do to move it a few inches at a time. By the time they had it afloat, they were both puffing heavily.

Although they were now positive that Stan was not going to come back, they waited a few more minutes before poling out into the lake to the place where the water was deep enough so they could start the big outboard.

"I'd like to know why his grandfather is so down on us," Del said as they slowly moved the boat. "We haven't been around here long enough to have made him mad at us."

"It seems to me that we should wonder why Dr. Mulligan is so down on us. He's made Okimaw think we are here to help Ron take Stan away from him, and I'm sure he doesn't believe it himself."

Del pulled thoughtfully at the lobe of his ear. What Doug had said was true. Dr. Mulligan was doing his best to turn Stan's grandfather against them and Ron. He must be telling Okimaw that Stanley would give up Indian ways and maybe even stop living with him if he listened to the American missionaries.

Del and Doug did well fishing that afternoon, or so it seemed to them. They caught six jacks, or young male salmon, the largest of which weighed eight pounds; and three walleyes.

But when they got home, Ron laughed at their string. "Is that the best you can do?"

"I haven't seen any other fish around here that're any bigger than these," Doug countered.

"We don't keep fingerlings. We wait until they're grown."

Robbie and his younger brother came out to look at their catch. "How come Del and Doug didn't keep the big ones, Dad?" he asked.

Ron laughed. "See, what'd I tell you? Even Robbie's disappointed in the fish you brought home."

Del flushed. "You told him to say that."

Darlene came out on the porch just then. "You'd better get those fish filleted, Ron, if you want me to fix them for supper.

CHAPTER 3

MORE OPPOSITION

Del and Doug planned to find Stanley Ross that evening and ask him about the fishing trip he skipped out on and find out if he knew what Dr. Mulligan had against them. However, by the time they finished supper and devotions, it was so late that they decided to wait until the following morning.

"Besides," Del said, "he'll be over for Sunday school tomorrow. We can see him then."

Doug nodded. Ron had said Stan always came to the service on Sunday; so they could call him into their bedroom and talk to him then.

They waited for him to come to Sunday school the next morning, but he did not show up. They sat on the front steps until Darlene came to the door and reminded them it was time for Sunday school to start.

"We'll be in when Stan gets here," Doug told her.

She noted the time. "He's usually here by now. I doubt that he's coming this morning."

Reluctantly, they went into the living room, where the others had gathered, and took seats near the door. They could not understand how Ron and Darlene could be content to work in a place like this, where so few responded. There were no men in the service, and only two women, in addition to the three teenagers and half a dozen younger kids.

In spite of the fact that the group was small, Ron conducted the service with the enthusiasm he would have put into leading a Sunday school of five hundred. He had the group singing lustily, if off key. A couple of younger kids repeated Bible verses, and they all joined in on the birthday song for the youngest girl in the group.

Del and Doug kept glancing at the door, but there was no sign of Stan. As soon as the service was over, they called Ron to one side to talk with him about it.

"I suppose something else came up today that he thought was a little more important than being here," was Ron's explanation.

The boys had to admit that that was entirely possible. After all, Stan was not a Christian. He could not be expected to feel the same about the church and Sunday school as they did. Still, they could not put aside that look of fear that gripped the Indian boy's features when he must have realized that his grandfather was watching them from the window.

"Do you suppose he's afraid to come?" Doug asked.

Ron frowned. "I doubt it. I've never known his grandfather to tell him where he could go or who he could be with."

The boys told him what had taken place. Listening, Ron scratched the side of his nose, and he nodded. Then he said, "I'm not at all surprised about Dr. Mulligan. He's as good as told me to my face that he feels that way. But I don't think Okimaw is all that opposed to us. He's the chief and the local medicine man, but I've never had any trouble with him. I don't think he feels that strongly against us."

Darlene joined them in time to hear what Ron was saying. "Maybe Stan's sick," she said. "You know, he does catch cold easily."

They talked about the Indian boy again at the dinner table, and it was decided that Del and Doug would go down to see him when they finished eating. Robbie wanted to go with them, but his mother would not let him.

"I'm sorry, Rob. You'll have to stay home so you can take your nap."

His lower lip trembled. "Aw–."

"You don't want to get sick, do you?"

"I never get to go anywhere with Del and Doug, or have any fun."

Doug reached over and rumpled his hair affectionately. "Don't you worry. One of these days your dad and Del and I will take you fishing with us."

The boy's eyes lit. "Really?"

"It's a promise."

Del and Doug went down to Oliver Okimaw's cabin that afternoon to ask about Stan. The arthritic old chief met them at the door, hatred written all over his face.

"We thought maybe Stan was sick or something," Del said, "so we came to see how he is."

The chief glared at them. "Stanley doesn't want to see you anymore! You go away and leave him alone! Don't you ever come back here again!"

The boys backed away from Oliver Okimaw almost involuntarily. It was not that they were afraid of him. He was so crippled with arthritis that even a child could have defied him without being afraid he might hurt him. But there was something about the piercing fire in his eyes that affected them both, something mysterious and authoritative. Okimaw commanded awe and respect from those he met, whether they liked him or not.

"You leave Stanley alone! Understand!"

The boys did not answer him.

"I don't want to see him with you again! If I do. you will be in plenty of trouble with me!"

With that, the old man seemed to be enveloped by the shadows as he inched backward. The harsh lines of his face blurred, and the anger in his eyes was hidden from view. Bony fingers reached for the door, and it creaked shut. Momentarily, all was silent.

Del and Doug stared questioningly after Stanley's grandfather.

"He was really uptight!" Doug exclaimed.

"Whatever gave you that idea?"

He shrugged. "You know, I don't believe he likes us." He stooped, picked up a stone, and pitched it into the placid water.

Del laughed briefly. "I'd call that something of an understatement. To tell you the truth, I think he'd like to scalp us."

They left the old Indian's log cabin and made their way to the Hudson Bay Store. It was a warm, sunny afternoon, and people were everywhere, gathered in small clusters, talking jovially, or sitting in the shade, enjoying the day. A few spoke to Del and Doug. Most of them only nodded.

The boys covered that section of the village carefully, but there was no sign of Stanley anywhere.

"I don't get it," Doug said, shaking his head. "He just disappeared."

Doug turned slowly and squinted out across the vast expanse of water. Stan had vanished as completely as though someone had snatched him up and transported him, bodily, to the moon. "I wonder why he's avoiding us."

"Yes, the way he acted yesterday morning, it's hard to believe. He sure seemed like he enjoyed being with us."

"Don't forget his grandfather," Doug continued. "He's got to live with him, you know."

Del had to agree with that. Stan had been as friendly as anyone could be, until he realized that his grandfather saw him with them. Then he had turned and fled.

They sauntered past the newly built icehouse and turned toward the lakeshore, where the brightly painted boats were pulled up on the beach, because it was Sunday. They were determined to find Stanley Ross in spite of the fact that they were sure he was doing his best to keep away from them. Their search took them along the water's edge to the last cabin in the village.

"We'd just as well go back to the house." Del's voice revealed his surrender. He was sure they were not going to locate their young friend.

They angled back toward Ron and Darlene's, going by several small cabins and some tents. They were almost at the missionary's home when Del chanced to turn in time to see Stan with a few guys about his own age, standing near the steps of the Hudson Bay Store.

He grasped his brother's arm and squeezed it.

"Stan's over there to our right." He spoke softly, although there was no one else close enough to hear what he was saying.

Doug turned casually and saw that Del was right.

Their Indian friend was talking with several boys he did not recognize.

"Think we should go over and talk to him?" Del asked.

Doug nodded. "If he'll talk to us."

It was obvious that the Indian boy had not seen them yet. They changed their course and walked down the hill in the direction of the Hudson Bay Store, trying hard to make the move seem casual and unplanned. They were still about thirty yards away from the cluster of boys when one of them looked up. He must have said something to the others. Stan's head came up, suddenly, and for an instant he glared at them. It seemed as though his entire being shuddered. Then he turned and hurried around the corner of the store building and out of sight.

Del and Doug stopped where they were. There was no use going on. They had Stan's answer.

The following morning, the boys helped Ron lay out and dig the footing for the addition to the house.

If the cement had been there, they could have finished the foundation that day, but since it was not, they had to quit at noon. They did not feel much like going fishing that afternoon, but there was nothing better to do.

They came back a couple of hours before dark. By the time they had the boat pulled up on shore and had their catch filleted, the gloom of night had crept in from the muskeg area, a mossy, marshy ground across the lake. Stan came to see them as they were washing up for dinner. He came into the house uneasily, glancing in one direction and then the other, to be sure no one saw him enter.

He spoke to the Davis boys briefly and went into the kitchen where Ron was sitting. The young missionary knew the ways of Stan's people enough to know that he had come for a specific purpose, but he waited until the boy was ready to tell him why he had come. Stan talked about everything else and did not mention the reason for his visit until he was ready to leave.

"I have to tell you about my grandfather," he blurted suddenly. "He doesn't like it that I come over here while Del and Doug are here. He tells me I have to stay away until they leave."

Ron eyed him questioningly. He had lived with the Cree people long enough to know there were many things about them that he had difficulty in figuring out, but he could not understand why old Okimaw would be so opposed to Del and Doug. They were both good boys and would not get Stan into trouble. Besides, even if they were the wrong kind for his grandson to be with, they had not been on the reserve long enough for the old Indian to find out anything about them.

Actually, it was not the way of the Indians to tell their sons or grandsons they could not be friends with certain other boys. That was not how they raised their children. Even if he had known the boys would have a bad influence on Stan, the chances were that Okimaw would not have said anything. There had to be another reason for the old man's opposition.

Finally, Ron spoke. "We don't want you to do something your grandfather doesn't want you to do."

Stan's temper flashed. "Nobody tells me what to do!" He stiffened. "I make my own friends!" Then his voice grew softer. "But he got so mad, he said I couldn't stay with him anymore if I came over here before Del and Doug go back home."

The boys nodded understandingly. They were glad he was not angry with them.

"I have to come and see you when he is gone." With that, Stan opened the screen door and stepped out into the night. When he was gone, they went into the living room, where Darlene and the younger boys were sitting.

"What did Stan want?" Robbie asked.

"Now, Robbie," his mother warned, "you know that doesn't concern you."

But the boy was not satisfied. "Who is it who won't let him be with Del and Doug? Was he talking about his grandfather?"

"Get along with you. It's time for you to be in bed."

"Was he?"

No one answered him. The less Robbie knew, the less likely it would be for him to innocently embarrass them later.

There was only one reason why Okimaw would be upset about Stan being with the boys, Ron decided. He was afraid his grandson would forsake the old ways of his people if he became a Christian.

The following day, Ron took Del and Doug with him back across the lake to see Gordon again. He had to talk with the trader about hauling the building supplies over to the mission house.

The trip proved to be disappointing.

"I'll get your stuff across the lake like I told you." Impatience crept into Gordon's voice. "But you're going to have to wait until I get things worked out. I've got everything around here to do alone." A plaintive tone crept into his voice. "It ain't as though I've got a lot of help. I've got to work it in, and that's going to take some time."

Ron was so anxious to get the lumber across the lake so the building could begin that it was all he could do to keep his own impatience in check. But it would not do any good to be short with Gordon. Trying to pressure the trader would not work either. Gordon was too accustomed to moving at his own pace. One of the reasons he had gone into the North was to get away from the pressures of city life. He had told Ron that often enough. He would move the lumber at his own convenience or not at all.

"I'd like to have you get it as soon as you can," Ron went on.

"That I will." He spoke so firmly Ron was surprised.

"I sure would like to have it *this week*."

Gordon's face grew stern. "I don't know whether I'll be able to do it that soon or not. I'll have to see how things go."

There was no use in pushing the matter any further. Gordon had made up his mind that he did not have time to haul the building supplies right away. As far as he was concerned, that settled the matter.

Back in the boat, Del asked Ron what he was going to do next.

"We'll wait a few days and give Gordon a little more time. If he doesn't get the stuff hauled by the time that we get the footings poured, we'll have to figure something out to get it over to our place ourselves."

DETECTIVE WORK

Del and Doug had a great deal of time to spend around the reserve in the next few days while they waited for Gordon to haul the material across the lake. They were fascinated by the way of life in the Canadian North and wandered endlessly through the village, stopping to inspect the toboggans that were still used by some of the less prosperous trappers. The more successful men had snowmobiles in crude sheds behind their homes, but there were still those who used dogs, the way their fathers and grandfathers had in years gone by.

They were also interested in the huge, flat-bottomed boats the commercial fishermen used, and they never tired of walking among them.

"I don't know why Ron waits around for Gordon to haul the material to us," Doug said. "He could borrow a couple of these boats and do it while Gordon's thinking about it."

"Darlene asked him that yesterday. I guess he's tried, but no one will rent him a boat. He can't even hire anyone to do it for him, as badly as some of the men need the money."

Doug turned in the direction of the Hudson Bay Store.

"I sure didn't think the people felt that way about him and Darlene. Hadn't they been writing letters to Danny and Kay telling them how much they enjoyed being with the people?"

"That was before Dr. Mulligan came around. He's the one who's getting everyone stirred up."

Doug stopped on the path and broke a twig from a nearby saskatoon bush. "And I sure don't know why. Neither Ron nor Darlene have done anything to him."

"I know that. Ron says he claims he doesn't have anything against them; that his only concern is for the Indians. He doesn't want to see them made over into replicas of white people. Dr. Mulligan claims he's only trying to keep Ron and Darlene from influencing them against their native customs."

Doug continued to mull over the unfriendly anthropologist. He finally said, "He can talk about wanting to protect the people all he wants to, but I don't buy it. I don't think he cares anything at all about them. And I don't think he's an anthropologist, either. If he was, we'd see him with the people a lot more than we do."

Del frowned. "Come to think of it, the only person we see him with is old Oliver Okimaw. He doesn't pay any attention to anyone else."

Silence hung between them for half a minute. "Maybe we should find out why," Doug said quietly.

"I can't say I'm too keen about messing around with him," Del answered, shivering.

"We've got to do *something* to help Ron."

His brother nodded. "It's not going to be easy, Doug. We really don't know a thing about Dr. Mulligan. We don't know where he comes from or how long he's going to be here or where he's going when he leaves. And I don't think anyone else does. The way I get it, he came here, got Okimaw's permission to live on the reserve, and has been here ever since."

They were still talking about the self-styled scientist and the mystery that surrounded him when they saw him approach Oliver Okimaw's place from the lake and disappear inside.

"There he goes again," Doug said. "I tell you, he's got some reason for spending so much time with the old chief."

"Like what?"

"I don't know, but you can bet a character like that guy isn't over at Okimaw's because he enjoys his company. He's got some other reason for being there, I'll bet."

During the next few days, Doug and Del tried to find out something about the stranger but were unsuccessful. They tried to pump information from the Hudson Bay Store manager and a few Indian men they were acquainted with. The people they talked to either did not know anything or seemed determined not to reveal anything they did know. When Del and Doug finally gave up, they knew no more than they did the first day they arrived on the reserve.

* * *

Ron and Darlene tried hard not to let it bother them, but they too were feeling the new opposition to them and their ministry that seemed to be taking root among the people. Most of the time, they were scarcely aware of it, but occasionally, it would show through. The attendance at services was down, and in a few homes, they no longer felt welcome.

One evening that week, Darlene talked with Ron and the Davis boys about it. "I can't understand it. We haven't had any trouble with anyone. And I don't think the people are angry with us, but they are acting so distant and unfriendly all of a sudden. It's as though they want us out of here."

Ron picked up his Bible. "I get the idea that they're uneasy about us," he said. "I can't help feeling they like us, but they act as though someone has told them they really can't trust us."

"And I know why," she retorted. "It's that Dr. Mulligan." Her resentment flared. "Things have been different here on the reserve since he came."

Doug spoke up. "Only it's like I told Del. For an anthropologist, he sure doesn't spend much time with the people. You don't see him around the village or with anyone except the old chief. That really bothers me."

Ron agreed with that observation.

No one had noticed that Robbie came into the room until he tugged at his dad's arm. "What's an an–anthroplogogist, Daddy?"

"He's a man who studies the way people live. You'd better get back to bed."

The boy, however, was not ready to go. "Why doesn't Dr. Mulligan like us?"

"We didn't say he doesn't like us, Rob."

"Yes, you did. You said he made the people change and not trust–."

"You get back to bed, young man," Ron ordered.

Protesting, Robbie got a glass of milk and went back to his room. When they were sure he was in the bedroom and the door was shut, Ron cautioned the others about talking in front of him. "He's just as apt to corner Dr. Mulligan and ask him why he doesn't like us as he is to talk to us about it. We've got to be more careful about what we say."

There was a short, taut silence. Then Doug spoke up quietly. "To tell you the truth, I'm sort of like

Robbie. I'd give a lot to ask Dr. Mulligan just what he's doing here."

"You don't think he'd tell you, do you?" Del asked. Then he turned to Ron. "Do you know what he could be up here for, if he's not an anthropologist?"

"Maybe he's a prospector."

The Davis boys had thought of a lot of things Dr. Mulligan could be, but they had never considered that possibility. "What does he think he's after, silver or gold?" Doug wanted to know.

"Or nickel or copper or some other valuable metal. But I really don't believe he's a prospector. Dr. Mulligan doesn't seem to be the type, as far as I can tell. He doesn't look rugged enough."

"Maybe he acts that way on purpose, to throw us off."

"I don't really care why he's here," Ron said, "as long as what he's doing is legal and he doesn't hurt us or the people."

Del and Doug had planned on going fishing the next morning, but they saw Dr. Mulligan pull away from the dock as they were leaving the house.

Doug turned quickly to his brother. "What do you say we follow him?" he whispered.

"Are you out of your mind?"

"What better way is there to find out what he's doing?"

Del balked at the idea of following the scientist. He did not seem like the kind of person who would welcome uninvited observation.

"As long as we don't have to get too close," he agreed, as a safe compromise. He could not let Doug think he was a little afraid of Dr. Mulligan.

They poled the mission boat away from the dock and started in the general direction Dr. Mulligan had gone. He was so far ahead of them and was traveling so much faster than they were that he was soon out of sight.

"Now, where do you suppose he went?" Doug asked.

"Search me," Del shrugged, trying to mask his relief.

"It's no wonder he didn't try to hide the fact that he's going across the lake. There isn't another boat on the reserve that's fast enough to catch him."

In spite of the fact that the scientist had completely eluded them, they went across the lake and began to poke, curiously, among the islands.

"And just what're we going to do if we do see him?" Del asked. "He's going to know we're trying to spy on him, and we can be in real trouble."

Doug picked up his fishing rod and dropped the lure into the water to start trolling. "We like to fish. Remember?"

Del followed his brother's example. "This might fool Dr. Mulligan," he said doubtfully, "but he's mighty sharp."

A thin crooked grin rested lightly on one corner of Doug's mouth. "The trouble with you is that you worry too much."

They spent the rest of the day trolling among the islands, keeping a watch out for Dr. Mulligan as they did so. They caught half a dozen nice jacks and were about ready to leave for home, when they heard the sudden snarl of a powerful outboard.

"Dr. Mulligan!"

Del jerked erect and stared in the direction the sound of the motor was coming from. An instant later, Dr. Mulligan's powerful boat zoomed into view. Both Del and Doug crouched tensely, making themselves as inconspicuous as possible, but that proved to be unnecessary. The man in the other boat was looking straight ahead; he seemed not to have seen them.

Still, they did not move until the other craft was out of sight.

"Well," Doug said, disappointment evident in his voice, "he's gone now."

"We came close to finding him!" Del exclaimed, only not with the same disappointment Doug had.

"I was just thinking that myself. If we'd only gone around the other side of this island, we might have found out what he's doing."

Del squinted at him. "Maybe it's a good thing we didn't," he retorted. "Did you ever think of that?"

He would have turned their boat back toward the reserve, following Dr. Mulligan across the big body of water, but Doug suggested that they wait for a time.

"If we come along right behind him, he's going to

spot us and be mighty suspicious. We'd better wait until he gets out of sight, at least."

Del had to admit that what Doug said made a lot of sense. Dr. Mulligan had acted as though he did not know they were within fifty miles of him, but they could not be sure of that. He could have seen them and pretended not to know they were there. If that was the case, they would have a lot better chance of making him think they were fishing if they stayed out for another hour.

"We'd just as well do some more fishing and let him get in and away from the dock before we go home," Del suggested.

"I've got a better idea."

"Like what?" Del eyed his brother suspiciously.

"We know Dr. Mulligan was ashore not too far from here. If we go over there, we just might be able to locate where he was and find out what he was doing."

Del groaned aloud. "I might have known you'd come up with an idea like that."

They went around the point of the island in the direction the mysterious scientist had come from. It did not take long to find the marks of Dr. Mulligan's boat on the sandy beach. "Anyone could see that a boat's been pulled up on the sand here recently," Doug said. "I don't think he even tried to hide his tracks."

"He probably didn't think anyone would be over this way for a while."

"Or maybe he doesn't want to give the impression that he's doing anything secret."

The boys had no difficulty following his path of broken twigs and here and there a clear footprint.

"I just happened to think of something," Del exclaimed.

Doug stopped and waited.

"You don't suppose he came over here to meet some-one, do you?" Del asked quietly but apprehensively.

"What difference would that make?"

"None. None at all – unless the guy is still on this island."

Doug shook his head. "You can think of the most pleasant things."

"Skip it. I didn't mean to get you uptight."

"Oh, no," Doug replied. "You wouldn't want to get me uptight. You wouldn't even try to do a thing like that, would you?"

"It always pays to keep thinking ahead."

They followed Dr. Mulligan's trail halfway across the island. It seemed that he had been looking for something. He had frequently turned to one side of the path or the other. But, if he was trying to find something special, the boys did not think he had found it. At least he kept right on going.

For another half hour, they followed Dr. Mulligan's path through the woods and muskeg, but without success. They were about to turn back when they came to a place where there had been digging.

"Hey! What's this?" Del exclaimed.

CHAPTER 5

FRIENDS IN NEED

Del was the first to reach the place where someone had been digging and bent over to examine the hole in the thick, black mud. "What do you make of it, Doug?"

"Nothing." He looked up. "Absolutely nothing. The roots here are so thick he couldn't dig more than a foot without using an ax. He should have known that before he started."

Del picked up a short section of root the thickness of his thumb. The sharp, clear marks of a knife or hand ax were still visible. "If he didn't know it before he started, he sure found it out in a hurry. He didn't dig very long."

Doug poked in the mud with a forefinger. "None of this makes sense. No sense at all."

Finally, disappointment clouding their faces,

they made their way back to the place where they had left the boat.

"Let's not say anything about this to Ron and Darlene," Doug said.

"Why not?"

"No real reason, except I can't see that it would help any. They might not appreciate our snooping around like this."

"Yeah," Del agreed, with a smile. "I can just see the look on Kay's face when Ron calls to say we got knocked over the head up here someplace."

When they got back to the reserve, Darlene and her sons were down at the dock. As soon as Robbie saw Del and Doug, he broke free of his mother's grasp and dashed to meet them.

"Robbie!" she called out.

But they were already at the dock, and he was so excited he did not hear her.

"Hi, guys!"

They spoke to him and reached out to tie the anchor rope to one of the heavy posts.

"Did you find out?"

They stared curiously at him. "Find out what?" Doug asked.

Del noticed a man crossing the beach near their dock, but he was more interested in what little Robbie might say.

"Did you find out what Dr. Mulligan was doing

across the lake? That's what Daddy said he thought you were going to do this afternoon."

The Davis boys colored. Looking beyond Robbie a few yards, they saw the tall, sinister scientist, a tantalizing smile playing on his lips.

"That's most interesting," Dr. Mulligan said, "I wasn't aware that I was playing a part in an intrigue. When you find out why I was fishing across the lake, I wish you'd tell Robbie. I wouldn't want him to think bad thoughts about me."

Then, laughing at some secret joke, he continued on his way.

"Now we are in for it!" Del groaned audibly.

Robbie turned his attention to the fish and was chattering excitedly about them. But the harm was done. Dr. Mulligan knew that Del and Doug were trying to find out what he was doing on the reserve. That would make things worse than they were before, and they could not do a thing about it.

Doug and Del did not see Stanley Ross for several days, and they decided he was trying to obey Okimaw so he would not have to leave his house. Finally, the Indian boy came to the mission house one night and announced that he wanted to take the boys fishing the next day. "That is, if you're not going to be working on the house tomorrow," he said.

"As a matter of fact, we will be pouring the foundation tomorrow," Doug said. "The plane came in with the cement this afternoon."

"But that won't take more than a day," Del broke in. "How about going out day after tomorrow?"

Stanley hesitated. "I think it will be alright. I'll have to see."

The Davis boys were eager to go fishing with Stan, but they were not sure if it was a good idea. He might feel they were encouraging him to go with them against the wishes of his grandfather. They looked at Ron.

"What will your grandfather think about it?" Ron asked.

Stan's temper blazed. "I run my own life."

"As long as you live with your grandfather, Stan, you should obey him," Ron reminded him.

"It's not grandfather! It's that Mulligan! He is the one who turns grandfather against you."

Ron ignored the reference to the other white man. "We should obey the Bible, even when it says something we don't like. And God tells us that we should obey those who are in authority over us." He paused to let that sink in, and then said. "And in your case, that means you should obey your grandfather."

The Indian boy stood near the door, his lips trembling. He did not argue with Ron. A well-mannered Cree did not raise his voice in argument, especially against someone older than himself. Still, it was apparent that he felt bad.

When he was gone, Doug turned to Ron.

"I wish we could've taken him along tomorrow.

We still haven't had the chance to go fishing with someone who really knows the lake."

"I'd like to have him go with you too," Ron replied, "but for a different reason. I think there would be a good chance that you would be able to lead him to Christ. He's younger than you are by a couple of years, so he looks up to you. Your example could be a big help to him." Ron paused. "But we have to honor Oliver Okimaw's feelings – at least until Stan gets a little older, old enough to be on his own. We can't tell the people they should live by the Bible and ignore it ourselves."

The next morning Del and Doug helped Ron mix and pour concrete for the foundation. After lunch, at Ron's suggestion, they went over to Gordon's at the south end of the lake to see if he would be able to do the hauling that day. He acted half insulted that the boys would even ask about it. "I *told* Orlis I wouldn't be able to get that stuff hauled for him until I got a little more time." Gordon's eyes narrowed. "If he's gettin' in too much of a hurry, he'd just better get someone else to haul it for him. I ain't got the time to do it for a week or so."

Once they were in the boat and out from shore far enough so they would not be overheard, Doug turned to his brother. "I don't think Gordon's ever going to haul those building supplies for Ron."

"He sure doesn't act like it. When we talked to

him just now, I got the same idea you did. He doesn't plan on doing it, so Ron had better get someone else."

"But who?" Doug wanted to know. "He told us he had tried to borrow or rent boats from the people on the reserve, but nobody would help him."

Del frowned. "You don't suppose Dr. Mulligan came over here and somehow made Gordon refuse to haul the stuff for Ron, do you?"

Doug had not thought about that, but it did make sense. It would not take much digging to find out that Gordon was one of the few who could get the building material across the lake. By talking Gordon and the Indians into refusing to help, Dr. Mulligan could stop the addition from being built for at least a year. But Doug could not see why Ron's two new rooms should concern Dr. Mulligan at all.

Del agreed with him and added that they had to do *something* to help Danny's younger brother and his family. Ron and Darlene had been living on the reserve for three years, and if they were unable to do anything about getting the lumber hauled, it was certain that he and Doug would probably do no better, but they knew they had to try.

Now that they knew about Gordon's decision not to haul the building supplies in the near future, they thought they should go home and tell Ron about it. They were threading their way between two islands a couple of miles from the south shore when they saw an Indian boat pulled up on one of them. Usually, when Del was running the boat, he only looked straight ahead. However, this time he chanced to see the brilliant crimson boat among the reeds.

"Look over there, Doug," he said. "Isn't that old Okimaw's boat?" He slowed down so his brother would have time to look. Just then, they saw the old Indian stagger up to the boat with the leg of a huge moose across his shoulders.

"It *is* Okimaw!" Doug exclaimed.

While they were watching, the old chief stumbled and almost fell.

"He shouldn't be lifting anything as heavy as that," Del exclaimed. "He's an old man! Let's go and help him."

"He'll run us off."

"Maybe, but we can try, anyway."

He headed the boat toward the island. By the time they reached shore, Oliver Okimaw had deposited the load of meat in his boat and was sitting on a log nearby, breathing heavily. His chest heaved, and the perspiration gleamed on his face. He eyed them wearily but did not speak.

"Hi," Doug called out cheerily. "Is everything alright?"

There was no answer.

"Are you alright?" he repeated.

"Why wouldn't I be?" the old Indian demanded irritably.

Del studied Okimaw's face. Fatigue had deepened

the lines in his gaunt face. He looked so worn out, Del was concerned for him. And he had only one quarter of the big animal carried back to the boat. If it was very far from the shore, Okimaw would never be able to get the rest of it to the boat. "Would you like to have us carry the rest of the meat out for you?" he asked.

Suspicion glittered in the old man's dark eyes. "You don't want to help me. I have no money to pay you."

"We don't expect to be paid. If you'll just tell us where the meat is, Doug and I will go and get it for you, won't we?" he added, looking toward Doug.

His brother nodded.

But Okimaw would not believe them. "Why should you want to do that for me?"

Del and Doug knew what he was thinking. He was sure they had their own reason for wanting to gain favor with him. That was the way of the white men he had been around. They never did anything for anyone else unless it was to their personal advantage. The boys did not blame him for not trusting them. He had no reason for thinking they were any different.

They sensed his hostility, and, in spite of themselves, felt their own tempers rising. They sensed that this was not the appropriate time to try to explain how the love of Christ makes Christians do nice things for people.

Doug spoke for both himself and his brother.

"You look as though you need help, and we don't have anything to do right now. We'll be glad to go get the meat for you if you want us to."

Okimaw did not want to accept their help. These were the two boys who had come to help the missionaries take Stanley away from him, to make him follow the white men's ways. On the other hand, he knew his own limitations. A few minutes ago, he had felt his heart hammering unevenly against his rib cage as he staggered under the load of the front quarter. More than once on the mile and a half carry, he had been sure his knees would buckle and he would go down under the load.

Even as he argued with the boys, he was dreading the rest of the task. He still had three more trips, and two of the loads would be even heavier than the front quarter he had just carried. For the first time since he had been hunting, he was afraid he would not be able to carry home his kill.

Okimaw knew better than to shoot a moose so far from the water. He should not even have gone out into the muskeg with his rifle, but it had been many weeks since anyone on the reserve had killed a moose; and, since he was the chief, the people looked to him at times like this. So he had gone across the lake into the dense muskeg and had killed the huge bull a mile and a half from the water.

He did not like the idea of accepting the help of the white boys. He did not trust them. But today he had no choice. He had to accept their help or leave the rest of the meat in the bush.

"I can give you some meat," he offered. That would be better than letting them help him for nothing.

They shook their heads. "You'll need it all."

"But I *have* to give you something!" he retorted.

"No, you don't. We'll go get your moose for you and it won't cost you anything." They did not realize how great was the old chief's pride.

The old Indian was sure they were lying to him, that sooner or later he would find that they had gotten something out of it for themselves. But it would be better to pay the price he knew the white boys would want from him than to risk losing the rest of the big moose.

Wearily he drew a map in the sand, showing them exactly where to find the moose.

"And be sure to come back *here*." His suspicion edged into the open once more. "It's the closest way to the lake."

CHAPTER 6

A FAVOR REPAID

Del and Doug left Oliver Okimaw sitting in the shade near his boat, still so exhausted he could not move, and went back into the bush to get the rest of the moose meat. They were glad the chief had drawn them a map, because with his keen knowledge of woodsmanship, he left behind a trail that only another person equally well trained could follow. To Del and Doug, there was no sign that the old Indian had used that trail.

Okimaw had told the boys it was almost a mile and a half back to the place where he had left the carcass of the bull moose, and they had thought he was exaggerating. It scarcely seemed likely that he could have carried one quarter of a big animal so far at his age. But after thirty minutes of steady walking they reached the place where Okimaw had butchered his kill. They stared incredulously at the two hindquarters and the remaining forequarter.

"That must've been the biggest moose in Canada," Del said in awe. "It's a good six feet from the shoulder down."

Doug lifted one of the huge pieces of meat and bone. "You're not going to get an argument out of me on that score. Old Okimaw could never have carried a whole hindquarter back to the lake. To tell you the truth, I don't see how he was able to make it with the other forequarter."

"He almost didn't make it," Del replied. "He's about done in right now."

The Davis boys each picked up a hindquarter and started back to the chief's boat. It took them more than twice as long to cover the mile and a half with their big loads. Even though they were young and in excellent physical shape, they were worn out when they reached the lakeshore.

"I'm sure glad we brought the heaviest loads this time," Del said. "I think I'd break down and cry if I knew we had to go back and get another load as heavy as this one."

Okimaw said nothing, but a weak and contemptuous smile appeared.

Doug saw it and got quickly to his feet. "Come on, Del, let's get with it. We've got another trip to make."

His brother squinted narrowly at him. "I thought we were going to rest a little while first."

"We can rest when we get back."

Still protesting, Del followed him into the bush. "Come on, Doug. What gives?"

"Didn't you see the way old Okimaw was looking at us? He was thinking that we're a lot softer than the Indian boys our age."

Del had not noticed the look on the chief's face, but he was sure Doug had read it right, and he agreed with him; he did not want the old Indian to think he and Doug could not do something the Cree boys their age could do. "It'll probably kill both of us," he muttered, "but we'll show him how wrong he was." They did not realize how great was their own pride either!

"You're such a stalwart soul."

"That's the truth, too, dear brother, but I sure hate to have to keep proving it all the time."

The trip with the lighter front quarter was much easier than the first. By taking turns, they were able to cover the distance to the Indian boat in only forty minutes.

"Well, here's the last of it," Doug said to Okimaw, with a wide smile. They put the meat in the bottom of the boat and spread the canvas over it.

Oliver Okimaw eyed them curiously. He expected the boys to try to bargain with him now. If they did, it would only show how stupid they were: they should have made a deal before they carried the meat. He did not care how much they protested; he was not going to give them anything.

Del and Doug said nothing about being paid, however; they did not even act as though they expected him to thank them.

"Your boat's going to be awfully heavy, Mr. Okimaw." Del said. "We'll push it back in the water for you."

He stood by, watching them questioningly, while they struggled with the heavily loaded boat. It was all they could do to get it into the lake again.

Once it was floating, Okimaw climbed in stiffly, without a word to them, and began to pole it into deep water. While the boys watched, he started his aged motor and angled across the lake in the direction of the reserve. He did not look back.

Doug expelled a long breath. "Well, that's over."

"And we didn't even get thanked." Del grinned crookedly. "What do you think of that?"

"I guess we didn't have any reason to expect him to thank us after the way he feels toward us," Doug said, "but we were able to help him. That's the main thing."

"I suppose you're right, but it would be good if he'd just acted as though he appreciated it."

They got in the mission boat and were soon following the old Indian's broad wake in the direction of the reserve.

Ron came down to the dock to meet them and

asked about Gordon and the lumber. "What did he say about getting the stuff over to us?"

"Well, he talked as though he still plans on doing it when he gets time, but he doesn't know when he'll get the time," Doug answered.

"We tried to push him a little," Del added, "and he said we'd have to haul it ourselves if we had to have it sooner than he can get around to hauling it for us."

"And it doesn't look as though he's ever going to get around to doing it," Ron said. For the first time, deep discouragement was reflected in his face.

"What can we do about it?" Doug asked.

"Right now, there's nothing we can do." He paused and turned, shading his eyes as he looked across the broad lake. "Do you realize the summer is getting away from us? If we aren't able to get the materials over here within the next few days, you're not going to be able to help us much."

The Davis boys had been thinking about that too. It gave them a helpless, frustrated feeling.

Ron Orlis went back to talk with the trader the following morning but was unable to get him to give a definite time when he could haul the supplies across the lake.

"I've already told you I can't do it until I get the time. If that isn't good enough for you, I guess you'll have to get somebody else to haul your lumber over to the reserve." He wiped his hands on the front of his shirt and leaned wearily on the counter. "A man c'n only do so much, Orlis. There ain't no way to crowd any more hours in the day."

Ron tried to hide his dismay. "I may have to get someone else."

Gordon shrugged. "Suit yourself. It don't mean nothing to me one way or the other. If you was wantin' to build something useful over there, I might feel different about it, but the people don't need *your* kind of religion. They've got one of their own."

Ron did not answer him. The truth was out now. Old Gordon had never intended to haul the lumber across the lake. The young missionary went back to his boat, discouragement weighing heavily against him. He had been on the reserve for three years without a convert – without one good friend. Maybe Dr. Mulligan was right. Maybe they should leave.

That evening, after Robbie and his younger brother had gone to bed, Ron and Darlene talked the matter over with Del and Doug.

"I've never felt quite so helpless," Ron said, "or so discouraged. There's no way I can think of to get our lumber over here, and we can't do a thing without it."

"Couldn't you go to the men who have big boats?" Darlene asked. "Surely there's somebody here who would help us."

He shook his head. "There's nobody who'll rent us their boats. I've already tried."

"It's that Dr. Mulligan," Doug said. "He's stirring up the people all the time."

That particular night, Ron was not ready to accept the fact that Dr. Mulligan was the root of their problems. "We've been here a lot longer than he has. We should have made at least *one* friend in three years." He paused. "I'm beginning to think that God didn't really call us here. We've got to be out of His will, or things wouldn't be as hard as they are."

"Ron!" Darlene exclaimed. "Don't say that!"

He looked up, exhaustion and deep despair reflected in his rugged features. "We've got to face reality, Darlene. We've been here more than three years, and what have we accomplished? We haven't even made one friend who likes us well enough to help us with a little job like getting our lumber over here."

"Nobody said it was going to be easy opening a work here."

"I know, but I'm beginning to think God doesn't want us here. If He did, He would be blessing our work with some results. As it is, He hasn't even helped us with a little thing like moving our building supplies across the lake."

Usually, Darlene was the weak one, but now she was strong and encouraging. "Maybe this is God's way of testing us, Ron," she said. "Maybe He wants us to depend more on Him. If He wants us to build the addition to our house this summer, He will help us, regardless of what the people say or do."

Her courage seemed to give him strength. "I'm

sorry, Darlene. I guess I was just feeling sorry for myself."

They were kneeling to pray when Stanley Ross came to the house, knocking boldly on the front door.

"Hi," he said, swaggering in triumphantly. "I thought I'd come over and see you for a while."

"Fine." Ron was about to ask him if his grandfather knew where he was, but he decided to wait.

"I came over to see Del and Doug. I can take them fishing tomorrow if they want to go."

"That's fine," the missionary answered, "but what about your grandfather? Did he say it would be alright?"

Stan nodded. "He sent me over here."

"Are you sure about that?" Ron asked doubtfully. It hardly seemed possible that such a thing could happen.

"That's right. He asked me to come over here. He said I can go fishing with the guys."

"That's great!" Doug exclaimed.

"And he wants to know if you need some boats to haul your building material across the lake. He might be able to help. .

Ron felt the color leave his cheeks, and his legs felt weak. He groped for the chair behind him. It was incredible! Oliver Okimaw had been opposed to him and his work from the start. The old chief had not even wanted to grant him permission to live on the reserve and had been disturbed when some of his council insisted on it. And lately, since Dr. Mulligan had been in the area talking against him and what he was trying to do among the people, the old chief's opposition had grown.

"You can't mean that!" he said weakly.

"It's the truth," Stan said firmly. "Grandfather said he knew Gordon was stalling you about hauling your building material over here. So he said I should come over and tell you that you can use his boat tomorrow. If you need any more, you're supposed to tell me. He'll see that you get them."

"Praise God!" Darlene murmured prayerfully.

"And we hadn't even prayed!" Del added, awe creeping into his voice. "We were just going to begin when Stan came."

"What does the Bible say about that?" Darlene asked Del. "He knows what we need, even before we ask."

The Indian boy eyed them blankly, bewildered by what they were saying.

Ron had to admit that God had worked in the old chief's heart. That was the only explanation. A man like Okimaw did not change so quickly on his own.

"What happened, Stanley?" he asked.

"I don't know. All I know is that he said I should come over and talk to you about using our boat. And he said I could be with Del and Doug any time I want to."

The Davis boys glanced quickly at each other. The rest of them did not know why Oliver Okimaw's attitude had changed, but they thought they did. "Do you suppose it could be because of the moose meat?" Del asked. Hurriedly, he related what had happened the day before.

Ron's eyes shone. "That had to be the means God used to bring Okimaw around. You guys helped him; now he wants to help us."

"But that doesn't mean that God hasn't worked in his heart," Darlene quickly added. "It's just as much an answer to prayer as if the lumber was miraculously transported over here."

"That's for sure," Ron murmured thankfully.

"Maybe it's even more of a miracle." She paused. "Maybe his attitude toward the gospel is changing."

Stan twisted nervously in his chair.

"Has it changed, Stanley?" the missionary asked.

"He told me I can't come to your Bible studies or to the meetings you have on Sunday," the boy explained. "If I do, I have to stay away from here." He brushed a hand nervously through his black hair. "Grandfather's ideas about Jesus aren't any different than they've ever been. I think he hates Him!"

Darlene seemed terribly disappointed. "I guess I was expecting too much."

"It would be wonderful to have him for us instead of against us, but at least he's going to help us get our lumber across the lake. That's a lot right now."

"It certainly is," his wife acknowledged. "And I think it's the answer to some of the things you were saying a little while ago about God not wanting us here."

CHAPTER 7

A WELL-ARRANGED ACCIDENT

The following morning, Stan Ross was at the Orlis home before the family had finished breakfast.

"I got the boats you wanted, Ron," he said. "Grandfather let me use his, and I got another one about the same size."

"Good. That's exactly what we need."

Ron was happier and more relaxed than he had been for months. After three years of work, there was a little crack in the indifference and opposition they had felt among the people on the reserve. It was only a sliver of light, but it showed them that God was with them, that He wanted the work to go forward.

They towed the two boats across the lake to the Gordon Trading Post. The old trader seemed disappointed that Ron was going to be able to haul the material himself. "I said I'd get around to hauling it as soon as I could," he protested. "You didn't have to get in such a hurry."

"We have to get started if we're going to have the addition finished this summer," the missionary explained. "We had a chance to borrow some boats, so I thought we'd get the stuff this morning."

"Suits me fine." The mask came back, and Gordon treated him with studied indifference. "It's just one more thing I won't have to do."

Stan and the Davis boys were already hard at work. They had carried some of the dimension lumber down to the boats and were improvising a barge, according to Ron's instructions. They made a platform of twenty two-by-fours and supported either end on the boats they had borrowed. Once that was accomplished, they carried the rest of the material down to the lake and loaded it. Ron soon came to help them.

Everything was going well, but it took longer to get the lumber loaded and tied down than they had supposed it would. It was almost noon before they were finally ready to cross the lake.

Doug glanced nervously up at the sky and then at Ron. "What do you think about the weather?" he asked. "Is it going to stay calm enough for us to make the crossing this afternoon?"

"It should be. I checked the forecast this morning before we left home. It sounded as though we're going to have excellent weather for the rest of the week."

"I sure hope so," the boy answered, his voice betraying his uneasiness.

"You sound as though you know something about the weather that I don't."

Doug laughed. "To tell you the truth, I don't know anything at all about it. I was just looking at that contraption we're going to be towing across the lake. If the wind comes up, it could give us a lot of trouble."

Ron hesitated, uneasiness gripping him for a moment. He had been concerned about the weather himself, in spite of the forecast, but they had been waiting for so long to get the lumber across the lake, he felt the slight risk was worth it.

"We've been praying that the weather would stay calm," he said aloud.

Before leaving the trading post for the long trip back across the lake, Ron checked the gas tanks on his regular outboard motor and the smaller kicker he carried for a spare. Then he joined the others already aboard his boat.

"Come on, let's go," he said. "It's a long way home. The sooner we get started, the sooner we'll be there."

None of them knew a great deal about pulling the makeshift barge, and it took some time to get the long line in place and adjusted properly so the heavy load would follow directly behind the boat. When they did start to move, it was only at a painfully slow crawl.

Gordon came out on the porch of his trading post

and called out to Ron, his voice booming above the muted throb of the outboard. "You'll never make it with that rig."

Ron waved to him and opened the throttle of the big outboard to drown out his voice.

Although he was running the motor at three-quarter throttle, they plowed heavily through the placid water. It seemed to Del and Doug that they were making but little more progress than when the motor was running at a fast idle.

Del turned to Ron. "We're not going to set any speed records, that's for sure."

"Won't it go any faster, Ron?" Doug asked. "It'll take us a week to get across the lake at this rate."

Ron shook his head. He wished they could pull the boats faster too, but there was no use in being impatient. No matter what they did, it was going to take several hours to cross the lake. They might just as well resign themselves to that fact and take it easy.

One hour dragged into two, and they still were a scant halfway across. The Davis boys and Stan were beginning to nod sleepily. Even Ron closed his eyes from time to time.

Doug was the first boy to notice that the wind was beginning to change. He felt the big boat lurch and he opened his eyes suddenly. The wind slapped his cheek and skittered across the smooth water, making little waves in it.

"Ron!" he cried. "The wind's coming up!"

The youthful missionary was already staring out across the wide expanse of water. The waves were getting higher, and here and there they saw one with an edge of foam.

"I don't think it's bad enough to cause us any trouble," Ron said calmly. But he was not sure he believed what he said. He knew the big lake and had seen how quickly it could be whipped to a frenzy in a matter of minutes. And they were not in a boat that could move fast enough to outrun the storm if it should develop. They were trapped at a creeping walk by the weight of their cumbersome cargo. There was nothing they could do except tough it out.

He opened the throttle slightly, even though he knew there was little chance of getting more speed. The boys said nothing, but they all sat up straighter and watched the growing waves. They were all concerned, but no one wanted to be the first to admit it. Del and Doug were praying silently, asking God to take care of them and help them to get their great load across the stormy lake.

They had been bouncing over the crescendoing waves for ten minutes when the big boat jerked violently over a huge breaker. Going up the wave, it slowed while the homemade barge sped faster, slackening in the line. At the crest of the wave, the boat picked up speed, suddenly, slamming the rope tight with a wild jerk.

It all happened in an instant. The boat was jerked

out of position by the sudden weight of the cargo, and a wave crashed into the bow. The 40-horse-power motor worked itself up on the transom, the transverse beam on the stern twisted, and went overboard.

"Ron!" Doug's shout of warning was lost in the roar of the wind.

For one tense, agonizing moment, the startled quartette stared at the rough water where the motor had disappeared.

"It's gone!" Del shouted above the deep-throated rumble of the wind and the breakers.

At that instant, Stan sprang to action. Grabbing a plastic oil bottle Del and Doug had rigged with a cord and weight to mark the spot where they found fish, he threw it out, as close as possible to the spot where the outboard had gone down.

Ron was struggling with the spare motor, bracing himself desperately against the frantic lurching of the boat. "Hey, you guys! Give me a hand!"

Del helped him with the motor while Doug and Stan snatched up the poles and used them to hold the heavily ladened cargo boats away from the mission craft. It seemed to take an hour to get the other motor fastened in place and the gas line hooked up, but it was only a matter of a few minutes.

Ron jerked the starter rope. The spare engine caught with a gratifying hum and slowly began to move the prow of the boat. The load was great for the small motor, but it was able to increase the distance between the powerboat and the others, until the line once more was taut. Again, they were under way, creeping uncertainly over the waves.

"Thank You, God!" Ron breathed prayerfully.

"I thought we were goners for sure." Doug exclaimed.

"You aren't the only one," Del said.

Stan Ross was as disturbed as they were. "We'd have been in big trouble if you hadn't had that extra motor along."

Ron shivered. He felt a twinge in his stomach as he realized the implications of Stan's words. The boy was right, and Ron was even more thankful for the spare. It was not large enough to move them very fast, but they were making progress. Without it, they would have had to cut the load of lumber free, not only losing the building material but the two boats as well.

He was furious with himself. Losing a kicker the way he lost this one was stupid. Any greenhorn should know enough to check the motor clamps and the safety chain. Then he knew he *had* checked them both that morning before leaving the reserve. He could remember it plainly. How could he have missed? Or, maybe he had not missed! Maybe – the thought was chilling. Maybe somebody had loosened the motor and had unhooked the chain.

He hated to think that anyone in the area disliked him so much he would do that sort of thing, but it was the only explanation. Ron glanced at his young companions, hoping they did not see the concern on his face.

The boat continued to struggle over one wave after another, so slowly, it seemed that they were making no progress at all. But as the hours passed, the trees on the opposite shore grew larger.

CHAPTER 8

STRONG MEDICINE

They were almost across the lake when Del asked the question that they all were thinking. "What about the motor, Ron? Are we going to be able to get it out of the lake?"

The missionary did not answer immediately. Fortunately, Stan had reacted quickly enough to mark the spot where the motor had gone down. At least they would be able to find the place again. The water must be fifty or sixty feet deep out there, however. Ron did not know of anyone who could go down that deep without scuba gear. And, as far as he knew, no one on the reserve would have any diving equipment. He doubted that they would have any chance of salvaging the motor, but he needed it desperately.

"I sure hope we will," Ron finally answered. Doubt

marred the usual confidence in his voice. "But it's not going to be easy."

Stan spoke up. "I think I know someone who can get it for us."

"Does he have diving gear? The water's deep out there, you know."

"I think he can get it for us," the Indian boy repeated.

"That would be great." It was plain that Ron did not share his assurance. "Who is he?"

"I'll have to go and see him," the boy continued. "He may not be diving anymore."

Once ashore, all thought of the lost motor was pushed temporarily aside. Oliver Okimaw came down to the dock and asked Ron if he needed help getting the material transported to the building site.

"Thanks, but I think we can get it. It'll just take us a little time."

"I have talked to some of the young men," the chief went on. "They'll help you."

Ron could scarcely believe Okimaw was volunteering to furnish help. It was so unlike the old chief.

Oliver Okimaw supplied the answer. "Your boys carried my moose out of the woods," he said quietly. "They were my friends." As far as he was concerned, that explained it.

Ron shot a quick, grateful glance at Del and Doug. "I'm glad they did, Oliver," he said gently.

The Indian stiffened at the use of his first name,

and when he spoke again, the hostility was back in his manner. "No one can say that Okimaw is ungrateful for any kindness shown him – even by a white man."

Ron was deeply disturbed at the old chief's belligerence. He had assumed because of the boats that Okimaw was softening. Now he saw that it was only a matter of honor. Del and Doug had been kind to him and would take nothing in return. Not to repay that kindness would be unworthy of a chief. He knew they would not accept money or meat, but they would accept the use of his boat.

In spite of the fact that it had started to rain, the men the chief supplied to help move the building material worked steadily until the last of it was carried up to the mission house. An hour before suppertime that evening, the last of the lumber was piled along the freshly poured foundation.

Darlene was excited about the prospect of getting started on the new rooms for their house. "Now we can get to work!" she exclaimed. "We're over the biggest hurdle."

"We hope," her husband said grimly.

"You shouldn't be that way, Ron. We should be happy things are beginning to work out for us."

"I would be, but I can't help thinking about the character who loosened that outboard for me so it would jump off the boat."

"Do you really think someone did a thing like that purposely?" Her tone revealed that she could not bring herself to believe that anyone on the reserve would hate them so much.

"It had to be done deliberately." Wearily he crossed the room to an easy chair and dropped his tired frame into it. "I checked both the safety chain and the clamps this morning before leaving the dock. They were just as secure as they had always been."

"Then how did it happen?"

"That's what I don't know. We were over at Gordon's, and we all went inside to talk to him before we started loading. That's the only time we left the boat and motor alone."

She pursed her lips a moment, and then said, "And you think somebody over there loosened the motor so it would jump off the boat while you were using it?"

"I hate to believe anyone would do that to us, but it's got to be that way. It's the only reasonable answer to what happened." He told her nothing more, but he was disturbed by more than the loss of the motor. An enemy who would cause him to lose his motor might do almost anything to hinder their work or cause them to get discouraged and leave. This might be only the beginning.

"Are we going to be able to get the motor out of the lake?" Darlene asked.

"I'm not sure. Even with a good diver and the proper scuba gear, it would be almost impossible to locate the motor and bring it up. It doesn't look too good."

* * *

Del and Doug knew how slim the chance was that the outboard motor could be retrieved from the bottom of the lake, and they knew what its loss would mean to Ron and Darlene. A motorboat for them was as important as a car to a country pastor. They had to have one if they were to get around to the people they should be visiting. The old kicker they used as a spare was far too small and unreliable to be. used regularly.

"How are Ron and Darlene going to get along without a good motor for their boat?" Doug asked when they were alone in their bedroom that evening.

Del moved to the window, looked out, and paused thoughtfully before he replied, "I sure don't know."

"They don't have money enough to buy another one. I heard Ron say they were spending everything they could spare on the addition to the house."

Del breathed deeply. He had not said anything to Doug or anyone else about his own suspicions regarding the motor and the way it just happened to fall off the boat while they were towing the lumber across the lake. He remembered seeing Ron check the engine and the safety chain just before they left the reserve that morning. That could only mean that someone had loosened the engine so it would come off when they were out in the lake.

Apparently, his brother had been thinking about

the same thing. "You don't suppose Stan's grandfather got somebody on the other side of the lake to make that kicker come off the boat, do you?" Doug spoke reluctantly; it was hard to put such an accusation into words.

Del shook his head. "He wouldn't do anything like that. He's not that kind."

"But he doesn't like having Ron and Darlene here. Stan told us Okimaw hates the gospel. He just might hate it enough to try to get Ron and Darlene to move."

"I still don't think he'd have any part in a deal like that," Del said. "He's an honorable man."

Doug had to admit that was true. "And he's the chief here. He really takes his position seriously. I can see him ordering us to leave, or making life unpleasant for us, but it would all be out in the open. He's not the kind to go sneaking around about anything."

"Maybe you're right," Doug answered.

"And besides," Del continued, "he wouldn't risk having his own boat damaged or ruined." He bent over and untied his shoes. "Somebody did it, all right, but not Oliver Okimaw. It's got to be someone else."

They finished undressing and crawled into bed.

"If it isn't Okimaw," Doug said, as they lay in the dark, "who's determined enough to stop Ron's work that he would do anything like this?"

Del had a name to suggest to his brother. "Did it occur to you that Dr. Mulligan just might be our man?"

Doug sat up. "Of course! Why didn't I think of him too!"

Dr. Mulligan was more bitterly opposed to Ron and Darlene than anyone else on the reserve – even more than Oliver Okimaw. He had done a lot of talking against them already, and had said some things that might be considered as threats.

"You could be right, at that."

They were just settling down to sleep when there was a commotion on the front steps.

"Ron! Darlene!" The young voice was hysterical. "Come quick!"

"That's Stan!" Doug exclaimed.

"What do you suppose he's doing over here at this hour?" Del asked, as they both scrambled out of bed.

"It's grandfather!" Stan was hammering on the door. "Come quick!"

Del jerked his trousers on and dashed to the front door. He flung it open half an instant before his brother got there.

"Stan!" he exclaimed. "What's wrong?"

In the pale light of the moon, he could see that the Indian boy's face was drawn with emotion.

"It's grandfather! He's sick. He's awful sick! You've got to help him!"

By this time, Ron was also at the door. "What seems to be the trouble?" Ron asked calmly.

"I–I don't know." Stan's chest was heaving.

"He–he–you've got to come! He's so sick I'm afraid he's going to die!"

Darlene joined them. "We'll go with you, Stanley," she said. "You can tell us about it on the way."

"That's a good idea." Ron ran back to the bedroom. "Let me get my shoes on, and I'll be ready to go."

"Hurry!" Stan said again. He turned and started down the steps to go back to the little cabin where he lived with his grandfather. "Hurry, Ron! You don't know how bad he is!"

Doug, Del, and Stan were out of sight already, but Darlene stopped Ron at the door. "Do you think the boys will be alright here alone?" she asked.

"Why?"

There was a concerned tone in her voice. "I don't like to leave them after–after what happened to you today. Would you stay with them?"

"Sure, I'll stay. You can probably do a lot more for Okimaw than I can. And if you need me, you can send one of the boys back for me."

Darlene had to run to catch the boys. Stanley Ross was half running in his haste to get back to his grandfather. The other boys were having difficulty in keeping up with him.

"Tell me what happened, Stan," Darlene asked, breathlessly.

Her voice had a calming effect on him, and he slowed to a fast walk. He was not puffing at all. "He hasn't been feeling good since he shot that moose and carried a front quarter out to the lake. He kept saying it didn't bother him any, but I knew better. He had a funny look, and a few times he said his chest hurt." A shudder ran through the boy's small frame. "It must've hurt him awful bad tonight. He woke me up and–and asked me to come up here and get you!"

Darlene was the one who quickened the pace as she learned more about the elderly chief's condition. She had taken a course in missionary nursing, so she guessed it was something like this. Oliver Okimaw still worked far too hard for a man of his age and physical condition. There was a prayer in her heart as she pushed open the little cabin door.

A faint, flickering kerosene lamp was struggling to chase away the darkness in the cabin.

"Mr. Okimaw?" She spoke softly, looking around as she did so. At first it was so dark in the corners of the little cabin that she could not see the old man. "Mr. Okimaw?"

Stanley pushed past her and hurried to the bed in the opposite corner. "Grandfather, I brought them," he said gently.

The old man on the bed stirred, a groan coming from his lips. Darlene was then able to see the small, dark form on the bed. She spoke quietly to him.

"Good evening, Mr. Okimaw. Stanley tells me that you don't feel so good." She pulled a chair up beside the bed and sat down, taking the old man's pulse.

It was erratic and fluttery, and so faint that she had difficulty counting it.

"How is he?" Stan whispered.

For the moment, Darlene ignored his tortured question. She really had no idea how sick the chief actually was, but she feared a heart attack.

"Do you have any pain?" she asked him.

Okimaw nodded once and gestured with his right hand toward his chest and left arm. "Across here," he said. His voice was so weak, she had to guess at the words.

She wished Ron were here to advise her. Even as that thought came, she realized what had to be done. Okimaw had to get medical help as quickly as possible. Even now, it might be too late.

Deliberately she turned to Del and Doug. "Go over and waken the Hudson Bay Store manager," she said crisply. "Tell him to radio for the mission plane."

"How does he do that?"

"He'll know. Go and tell him."

While the boys were gone, Oliver Okimaw opened his eyes and looked about, gesturing in the direction of the stove. It was obvious that he wanted something, but Darlene did not know what.

"Do you know what he's trying to say, Stan?" she asked.

The boy came over to his grandfather's bed and whispered to him in Cree. The old man said a word or two, and the boy turned to the stove and poured him a cup of strong tea.

"Do you think he wants *that?*" Darlene wanted to know. It seemed incredible that one so ill would want something that strong to drink.

"It is what he wants," the boy answered. "He fixed some tonight before he went to bed and drank two cups of it."

"It's so black." She shuddered. "I don't think he should have anything as strong as that – especially now."

"It's something he mixes up himself. He won't even tell me what's in it. But that's what he wants." With that, the boy gave the tea to his grandfather.

Darlene was surprised to see that the old Indian drank half the liquid in the cup without stopping, as though getting it down was most important. When it seemed that he could not drink anymore, he paused, breathing wearily, closing his eyes.

She started to take the cup away, but he reached out and grasped her hand with his shaky fingers.

"No!" he said as forcefully as he could.

"Do you want more?"

He nodded and struggled to raise himself on one elbow.

"Don't do that. I'll help you."

She managed to hold the cup in such a way that he could finish the rest of the tea in it. The effort seemed to exhaust him, and he sagged back on the pillow, and for a time, lay motionless. Only the slight moving of the blanket revealed that he was breathing. Darlene glanced at her watch and then at the door. Doug and Del should be back from the Hudson Bay Store by this time. She wondered what was taking them so long. Then she realized it was only her own concern that made her think the time was dragging.

Darlene was still sitting beside Oliver Okimaw's bed when Del and Doug came back a few minutes later. The Hudson Bay Store manager had gotten the mission by radio.

"Dick will be coming in as soon as he can after daylight," Doug said.

"That'll be in time, won't it?" Del asked with concern.

"I'm sure it will." She hoped she sounded more positive than she really was.

Oliver Okimaw seemed to be resting a bit easier, but he was so frail and his face so colorless, that Darlene was concerned that he might not make it through the night.

"Is there anything we can do?" Doug asked.

It was then that Darlene thought of Ron. She knew how disturbed he must be. Besides, she would like to have him see the old man. He might know more about his condition than she did.

"Would you mind going back to the house and staying with the boys so Ron can come?" she asked. "I'd like to have him see Mr. Okimaw."

They really did not want to leave the old Indian's cabin, but they could not turn Darlene down. Anyway, there was nothing they could do for Stan's grandfather, except to pray.

Ron questioned the boys at length about Oliver Okimaw before leaving for the cabin, and he wanted to know how soon the mission plane would be in after him.

"Dick said he'd leave as soon as it gets light enough for him to take off in the morning," Del said.

"Fine. Time means everything in cases like this."

Ron put on a jacket and hurried down to the little Indian cabin near the lake. He doubted that there was anything he could do to help the chief, but he could be there with Darlene, and show Oliver and Stan that they honestly cared what happened to the old man.

Okimaw was lying very still with his eyes closed when Ron opened the cabin door and slipped in. For a moment, he stood just inside the little cabin, staring intently at the slight figure on the bed. He had always thought Oliver Okimaw was small. Now, however, the Indian chief looked scarcely bigger than a child. Only his wrinkled face and sunken eyes betrayed his age.

"How is he?" he asked, speaking so softly he scarcely mouthed the words.

Darlene shook her head. She was not sure whether there was a change in the old man's condition or not. It seemed to her that he might be slightly better. The last time she took his pulse, it seemed stronger and more regular. Still, she did not want to say anything that might mislead Stan into thinking his grandfather was better or worse than he was.

Ron reached down and took Okimaw's pulse. He was surprised that it was so strong and took it again, thoughtfully.

"What do you think?" she asked.

"This is the first time I've seen him, but his pulse does seem to be stronger than I expected it to be."

Stanley's eyes brightened. "Do you think he's getting better?" he asked hopefully.

"I didn't say that," Ron told him. "I wouldn't know whether he's getting any better or not. His pulse just seems stronger than I thought it would be, that's all."

He pulled out another crude, handmade chair and sat down beside the bed. "We'll just have to wait and see."

Stan sat back, uneasily, and for an hour or more, he said nothing. Every few minutes, Ron or Darlene took Okimaw's pulse, and when the old Indian roused enough to want more tea, she gave it to him.

"Do you think it's alright for him to have that?" Ron asked.

"I don't see why it should hurt. It's strong enough to take the hair off a moose, but he seems to like it, and it hasn't done him any harm so far."

"It's medicine," Stan told them. "Grandfather mixes it himself. He says he's cured himself with it four times. It's good heart medicine."

Ron Orlis did not place much confidence in the old chief's private medicine, but he did not criticize it. If it would help Stan to think his grandfather was getting help from the bitter tea he was drinking, then there was no harm in it. It was better than having him believe his grandfather was getting no help at all.

Toward morning, Ron was quite sure Oliver Okimaw was beginning to improve. His pulse had slowed and was more even and markedly stronger. He asked Darlene to check it again, just to be sure.

She agreed with him. "There isn't any doubt about it. He's much stronger than he was even a couple of hours ago."

"We can praise the Lord for that," Ron said.

"What about the plane?" his wife wanted to know. "Do you think he still should go down to the hospital?"

"I think so. Don't you?"

Okimaw disagreed. "I'm getting well," he informed them. "I'll be alright before the plane even gets here."

"Maybe so, but you've had a bad sick spell. I really think the doctor should examine you."

The old Indian's voice raised. "I am the chief! What I say is what we do. And I say that I stay here!"

Ron saw that it would be useless to try to persuade him to change his mind.

"I'd better get over to the Hudson Bay Store and see if we can catch Dick before he takes off," he said.

CHAPTER 9

WET RESCUE

Old Oliver Okimaw wanted to get up immediately, but Darlene persuaded him to stay in bed a few days.

"I feel alright," he protested. "I feel fine."

"I'm sure you do, but we want to see you stay that way," Ron replied.

"You don't have to worry about me." He seemed embarrassed that Darlene and Ron had spent so much time at his little cabin. "You can go home now. Stanley will take care of me fine."

Darlene took his gnarled hand in hers. "We'd like to help you," she told him, "if it's alright."

He nodded grudgingly. "But I have to get up tomorrow. I have to go fishing."

"You'd better let somebody else do the fishing for a while," Ron put in, "until you get to feeling a little better. You don't want to get sick again."

Okimaw lay back on the pillow and closed his eyes. In spite of his protests to the contrary, it was obvious that he did not feel like getting up and doing anything.

"We'll come over and fix the meals for you and Stanley," Darlene told him. "And we'll help you what we can to take care of the other things you have to do."

He nodded wearily.

They continued to look in on him regularly. It was surprising to see how well he was doing. It was obvious that he was getting stronger. A few days later, Ron and Darlene found Okimaw sitting up, a cup of tea in his hand.

"You're looking good today, Oliver," Ron told him.

The chief's watery eyes squinted narrowly at him. "Why shouldn't 1?"

"I guess there isn't any reason why you shouldn't. And we're real glad to see how well you look. You'll be out of bed in no time."

"You laugh at Indian medicine, but it fixes me up fine." The old arrogance was creeping back. "Look at me. Does your medicine make a heart well so quick?"

Ron did not reply.

Stan waited just inside the door until Darlene gave Okimaw the soup she had prepared for him. She sat beside the elderly chief, talking to him while he ate.

It seemed to her that he ate better when he had company, and she was anxious to see him well. Stan motioned for Ron to come outside with him.

"What is it?" the youthful missionary asked. He thought the boy was going to ask or tell him something about his grandfather, but that was not the case.

"Did you get anyone to help you find your motor and get it out of the lake?" he asked.

Ron shook his head. Actually, he had been so concerned about Okimaw and getting the additional rooms built on their house that he had not thought much about the missing outboard motor, except to mentally write it off as a complete loss.

"I'll get someone to dive for it if you want me to," Stanley said.

Ron did not want to contradict the Indian boy, but he was sure it was useless to think that anyone could dive for the motor. It had gone down in fifty or sixty feet of water. He was sure there was no one around the reserve who would even try to go that deep, and he knew no one who had all the proper equipment. He could swim and dive quite well himself and he knew he would not want to attempt it without scuba gear.

"I'm afraid that's impossible, Stan," he said, gently. After all, the boy only wanted to help. He was not trying to build up Ron's hopes. "It's much too deep for free diving."

"But I'm not talking about free diving." Stan's voice raised insistently. "The field officer at Pine River has some scuba gear. He can go down and find your outboard motor easy. I know he can."

Hope flickered faintly in Ron's heart. "Hal Edgren? Are you sure he has diving gear?"

"I've seen him dive," the boy replied simply.

Ron straightened, staring out across the lake in the general direction of the place where the big outboard motor went down. For the first time, he began to feel that there might be a chance of locating the motor and bringing it up.

"Why didn't you say something about it before?" he asked.

"I was going to talk to him about it first. I wanted to see if he could do it. Then, when grandfather got sick–." He shrugged apologetically to show that he had completely forgotten about the outboard motor.

"Do you think he'll come?"

"He will come for my grandfather," Stan went on. "Grandfather is the chief, and he's done some favors for Hal Edgren. He'll come if my grandfather wants him to."

They went back inside, and Stan told Okimaw about Ron's outboard and wanting to get the Pine River field officer to come over and dive for it.

The old chief nodded to indicate his approval. "You go with him, Stanley. Tell Edgren that I want him to come over and bring that machine he dives with. He will come," he added confidently. "He will come."

Ron took Stan and the Davis boys that afternoon and they went in Okimaw's boat over to Pine River to see the field officer. Hal Edgren acted as though he could not spare the time to come over and dive for the motor, until Stanley mentioned his grandfather.'

"Did Okimaw send you over to talk to me?" the officer asked.

"He told me to come and ask you to do it. He's my grandfather."

"And what is it you wanted?"

Ron repeated the request.

The field officer noted the time. "I've never been busier," he said. "I really shouldn't take the time to go over and dive for your motor." A crooked grin appeared at the corner of his mouth. "To tell you the truth, Orlis, you've got quite a man in your corner. Oliver Okimaw is the only person in the North that I'd do it for. But he's been a true friend to me when I really needed a friend. Because of him, I'll do it."

At first, Ron suggested that Mr. Edgren go back with them, but as they discussed the matter, it was decided that he would come early the next day.

"That'll give me time to go over my gear and see that it's in shape before I come," he said, "and I'll have time to dive for your motor and still get back here before dark tomorrow evening."

On the way home, Del turned to Stan, curiously. "He sure thinks a lot of your grandfather."

The boy sat up straighter in the boat. "Everybody does," he said proudly.

The following day, the boys had just started to work on the building project, when a large, fast boat roared up the lake and nosed into the government dock. Stan, who was helping them, recognized it, even from that distance.

"It's Mr. Edgren!" he exclaimed. "He's come to dive for the motor."

Ron and the Davis boys went down to meet the field officer with Stanley.

"This morning looked so nice and calm I thought I'd better get over here a little early," he explained. "Are you all set?"

"All set," Ron answered happily.

They all climbed into his cabin cruiser. He touched the starter button and backed effortlessly away from the heavy piling.

"Now, tell me where to go."

In the fast inboard-outboard, going out to the place where they lost the motor was only a matter of minutes. It took them somewhat longer, however, to locate the marker. Del and Doug were both about ready to give up finding it when Stan saw the flash of red a couple of hundred yards away.

"There it is!" he cried.

Mr. Edgren turned the boat in that direction. "Are you sure?"

"It's got to be," Ron said. "There wouldn't be another red bottle floating way out here."

They went over to it and dropped anchor. Nobody said much, but Ron and the Davis boys were praying silently that the anchor on the plastic bottle would not have drifted far.

Mr. Edgren squirmed into his wet suit, and Del and Doug helped strap his scuba tank to his back.

"I'll go down and take a look first. "When I find it, I'll come back for the line," he said, with a gesture toward a coil of nylon rope. Then he slipped over the side of the boat and into the depths of the clear, cold water.

For several minutes, the tense little group waited, staring into the water at the spot where the diver went in.

"Do you think he'll find it, Ron?" Doug asked.

"We'll soon know," the missionary answered. Although he did not express his inner fears, he doubted seriously that the diver would be able to locate the outboard motor.

The minutes ticked away slowly. Nobody felt like talking. At last Stanley spoke. "If he was going to find it, he'd have had it by this time, wouldn't he, Ron?" he asked.

"I'm not sure. Don't forget, the wind was blowing hard when we lost the motor off the boat and you threw out the marker. We could have drifted some distance before you got the marker in the water."

"And the weight might have drifted a little bit more too," Del added. "Don't forget that."

"I think you're right. Anyway, we can't give up yet. We've just started to look for it," Ron said with more optimism than he felt.

"But Mr. Edgren can't stay around here very long," Doug said. "He's already told us that. If he doesn't find the motor soon, he'll have to leave."

As if in answer to their anxiety, the scuba diver came slowly to the surface and spit out the mouthpiece.

"Did you find it?" Stan called out.

Hal Edgren was grinning. "That's what I came to do, isn't it?"

He climbed into the boat and stretched out to rest for a couple of minutes. They watched him anxiously and waited for him to tell them more.

When he got his wind back, he continued. "We're about fifty yards away from it." He sat up and pointed. "It's right over there."

Del and Doug breathed prayers of thanksgiving.

"Think you'll have any trouble getting a rope on it?" Ron asked.

The diver shook his head. "It shouldn't be any problem. As soon as I get my breath, I'll take the line down and tie it to the engine." He took a few more deep breaths. "I'll give a couple of jerks on it when I'm ready, and you can pull it up."

They did as he directed.

It was only a matter of minutes until they had the outboard motor in the boat.

Ron grinned broadly and patted the dripping motor. "I sure didn't think I'd ever see that baby again."

Hal Edgren looked at it. "I know how you feel. It's a mighty good motor to lose."

"You can say that again."

Ron tried to pay him for coming over and diving for the motor, but the officer refused to take any money.

"I did it for Okimaw," he retorted. "He's one of the finest Indian gentlemen I've ever known."

On the way back to the reserve, Ron and the field officer discussed the "drowned" motor and what should be done with it.

"You're going to have to find somebody who can take it apart immediately and clean it up, Orlis. If you don't, it could be ruined anyway."

"I'm aware of that. I was just trying to decide whether to tackle the job myself or not."

"Why don't you let me take it back to Pine River with me? The department has an excellent mechanic stationed there, and he's always got some free time this time of year. If anyone can repair it, he can. But I'm not making any promises."

Once they were back at the reserve, Hal Edgren went to Okimaw's cabin to see the ailing chief. Ron and the boys went with him.

"Hello, Oliver," he said cheerfully.

The old man's face was ashen, and he trembled with rage. For an instant, he was so angry, he could not talk.

"What's the matter, Oliver? What's wrong?"

"She stole it!" the old man rasped.

The field officer did not think he had heard the old Indian correctly. "She what?"

"That woman!" He pointed a quavering finger at Ron. "That man's wife came here pretending to be my friend, and she stole the root for my heart medicine!"

CHAPTER 10

A THEFT

Oliver Okimaw glared at Ron, his rising hostility shaking his frail shoulders and making him breathe hard. He limped forward painfully to stand close to the young missionary. His rage seemed to increase his stature, and Ron, stunned by the sudden attack, retreated a half step. Before anyone else could speak, the old chief lashed out again wildly.

"And I trusted you both! You called yourselves my friends!" The words had the bite of profanity.

"I don't even know what you are talking about, Okimaw!" Ron exclaimed. "Darlene and I haven't stolen anything from you!"

"Don't expect me to believe that! I have already been deceived by your lies." He spat contemptuously on the dirt floor at Ron's feet. "You pretended to come here to help me, but like the wolverine, you only came to steal!"

Hal Edgren, who had been as shocked as Ron and the Davis boys by Okimaw's bitter accusation, spoke up calmly. "Now, Oliver. You've just been sick. You shouldn't let yourself get worked up like this. If anyone has stolen anything from you, we'll find out about it and see that they're punished. There's no need to get so upset."

"But she *pretended* to be my friend. She came over here saying she wanted to help me, and all the time she was a thief!"

"Now wait a minute, Oliver!" Ron broke in. "Darlene has never stolen anything in her life! I won't have anyone accuse her of stealing!"

Hal Edgren put out a restraining arm. "Take it easy, Ron," he said softly. "I'd better handle this. Right now, Oliver won't listen to you."

Reluctantly, Ron fell silent. Del and Doug knew that he wouldn't have been half so upset had the chief accused *him* of stealing, but he would not let anyone say anything against his wife. They had seen that when they had started teasing her and he thought that they were going too far, or that their remarks wore a cutting edge.

The boys could not quite understand what the old chief was saying, or why he was so sure Darlene had stolen from him. They knew her well enough to know that she had not; no matter how badly she wanted his roots, she would not have taken them. And she never wanted them. She really had no confidence in the medicine he had brewed. All she said about it at home was that it was so bitter she did not see how he could have swallowed it.

The field officer talked to the elderly Indian chief until he was able to calm him and induce him to lie down. "You aren't completely well yet, Oliver," he said. "If you aren't careful, you may have another sick spell."

Okimaw protested that he was alright, except for the fact that they had stolen his roots, but at Mr. Edgren's insistence, he allowed himself to be helped back to the bed where he lay down.

"But she took my medicine, I tell you! You've got to get it back for me," he pleaded.

The field officer sat down beside the bed. "I'm not sure she did steal your roots, Oliver," he said. "This young man doesn't seem to be the kind."

"That's the way they fooled me!"

"I don't think you've got any real evidence that she took anything from your cabin. You think she did, but that's not enough to make a charge against anyone. I know you're a fair man. You wouldn't want to accuse an innocent person of stealing, would you?"

Mr. Edgren's doubt seemed to hurt the old Indian, and for a time, he fell silent. "She's the only one who could have done it," he finally muttered defensively. "She took my medicine when she came down here to fix me something to eat this morning." Voicing the charge once more seemed to lend strength to it in his eyes, and his voice rose. "She *had* to be the one! No one else came to see me! She stole my roots!"

Ron could keep quiet no longer. "I can't let you keep on saying things like that about my wife when I know they're not true." He controlled his voice so he would not upset the old Indian more than he was already. "Del," he said, glancing at the boys, "go up and ask her to come down here right away. We've got to get this mess straightened out."

Del scurried out the door, and Doug was a half-step behind him. Okimaw saw that Stanley went with them and called imperiously for him to come back, but he ignored his grandfather.

As Stan hurried up to the mission house with Del and Doug, they both turned to him. "I don't know why your grandfather keeps insisting that Darlene stole his medicine," Doug said. "I don't think she ever took anything that didn't belong to her in her whole life."

"That's exactly right," Del added. "If your grandfather knew her the way we do, he wouldn't even *think* anything like that about her. She's not a thief."

Stanley agreed with them. "But I'm not the one who's got to have the proof," he countered. "Nothing's going to change grandfather's mind. When he makes up his mind about something, that's it! You don't talk him out of it!"

They walked half the distance to the mission house in silence. Del was turning the entire matter over in his mind. Old Okimaw had some reason for believing Darlene took his roots, even though they all knew she had not. If they were not gone, he would not have said anything. "Something must have happened to those roots, or your grandfather wouldn't think they'd been stolen," he said aloud.

Doug took up another possibility. "Do you suppose they could have fallen behind something?"

Stan shook his head. "That might happen with anything else he owns, but not his medicine. He keeps a close watch over those precious roots of his. They aren't in the house, or he'd find them." The boy's voice sounded resigned. "If grandfather says they're stolen, they're stolen. That's all there is to it."

Del and Doug told Darlene that Ron wanted her to go down to the Okimaw's cabin right away. They did not want to tell her the reason, but she insisted on knowing why she had to come right then. Del explained what had happened.

They thought she would be angry with Okimaw, but she said, "The poor man!" as she pulled on a warm sweater. "I know how much that medicine means to him. He must be frantic."

"And he says *you* took it!" Doug repeated, as though she had missed that vital piece of information.

"I didn't, of course," she answered simply, "but I can see why he might think that. I was one of the few people who came to see him when he was ill."

She went over to the neighbors and asked their

teenage daughter to stay with her two boys for a few minutes.

"I guess I'm ready now," she told her young companions.

They had gone only a short distance when Del paused on the path.

"What are you looking at?" his brother asked.

"That big plane on the lake. I've never seen such a big one up here."

"That's a twin-engine Canso," Stanley explained. "It comes in here all the time. Brings in supplies to the Hudson Bay Store."

As they watched, the clumsy flying boat inched closer to the government dock in front of the store. A dozen men were waiting to help with the unloading, while a couple of dozen women and kids and older men clustered on the steps, watching.

Darlene had gone on and was several yards ahead of them before the boys started forward once more. Del and Doug's thoughts turned back to the tense scene they had just witnessed in the Okimaw cabin, and they walked on faster.

"I sure hope Ron and Mr. Edgren are able to get this taken care of," Del said.

"Me too."

Stan, however, had not even heard them. He stopped once more and was staring down the grassy slope. "Is there anything that looks different to you down there?"

"Where they're unloading that plane?" Doug asked.

The Indian boy shook his head. "No, I wasn't looking at that. Over there." He pointed to the left of the Hudson Bay Store.

At first, neither of the Davis boys could see anything that was different than it had been since they arrived on the reserve a few weeks before.

"What is it?" Del asked.

"I don't know for sure, but something down there is different," Stan replied quietly.

Doug was the first to realize what Stan was talking about. "Dr. Mulligan's green tent is gone!"

"That's right! That's what I was missing. His tent isn't there anymore." His gaze was still riveted to the place where the American had pitched his tent. "I knew there was something out of place, but I couldn't figure out what it was."

Del took a step forward, speculatively. He certainly had not expected this to happen. "I thought he was going to stay here for another month at least."

"So did I," Stan replied. "He told grandfather the night before his sick spell, that his research was far from finished. And now–." He shrugged.

"The tent hasn't been gone very long, has it?" Doug wondered.

Del scratched his head and tried to remember. "I'm sure it was here yesterday."

"It must have been here this morning when we went out to look for the motor," Doug added. "If it hadn't been, I'm sure one of us would have noticed it as we left the dock."

Stan strode forward with determined steps. He called back, "I don't know about you guys, but I'm going over there where he had his tent pitched. Maybe we can find out something by looking around or talking to some people."

Del and Doug would rather have gone down to the cabin to learn what was happening there, but they seemed to be drawn irresistibly to the place where Dr. Mulligan had so recently had his tent set up. Stan's idea of talking to the people sounded alright to Doug, but he did not know what they could learn by looking at the place where the tent had been pitched. It was gone. That was all there was to it. But both Del and Stan seemed to think there was something to be gained by it, so he went along.

They examined the site hurriedly.

"He took the tent down only a few hours ago," Stan said, pointing to the still moist dirt that had been pulled up with the stakes.

"Why would he leave so suddenly?" Doug asked. "That's what I'd like to know."

Del squinted narrowly. He was thinking of what he and Doug had found that day they followed Mulligan's trail on the island across the lake. He had been digging for something over there and had stopped after taking out a few roots. Nothing had made sense then. Now he began to wonder whether it was significant or not. There was a possibility that it fit together.

"You don't suppose Dr. Mulligan's the one who stole your grandfather's heart medicine, do you, Stan?"

"Why would he?" the Indian boy demanded.

"Search me. But it does fit with something Doug and I learned about him a week or so ago."

His brother's eyes widened. "That's right! I'd forgotten all about that!" Hurriedly, he told Stan about seeing Dr. Mulligan across the lake and how they had located the place he took his boat ashore and where he went to the center of the island, digging for something. They did not know he was after only roots.

"What makes you think it was the medicine he was after?"

"He dug out a few roots," Doug explained.

"And there was no other reason he'd have dug where he did. The trees and brush were so thick the ground was a tangle of roots." Del paused. "The way I figure it, he was trying to get friendly enough with your grandfather to find out something about his roots so he could find them himself. When he couldn't locate any, he stole those in the cabin and took down his tent to get out of here."

"But why?" Stan persisted. "What would he do with it?"

Doug kept his eyes on the Canso, and answered, "If that heart medicine is as good as your grandfather says it is, maybe he was planning to sell it to somebody."

"Grandfather did show him the roots," Stan acknowledged. "And Dr. Mulligan asked a lot of questions about them, but he said he was interested in them because of his research on our culture. He claimed that he didn't know anything about plants."

Excitement glittered hotly in Del's black eyes.

"And he's one guy who visited your grandfather regularly. Did you ever think of that?"

"That could also explain why he's been so hostile to us. If he were friendly, we might hang around him too much and find out he's no anthropologist at all." The other two nodded their agreement with Doug's reasoning.

The more they considered the matter, the more neatly the pieces fit together.

"Only, how did he get out of here so fast?" Stan asked.

CHAPTER 11

TRUE CONFESSION

Del's mouth tightened grimly. It sounded just like Dr. Mulligan to steal those roots so cleverly that Darlene would be blamed for it. And all the time he was passing himself off as the best friend the old chief had. And to think, he had managed to get away! It made the boy furious. "Maybe an aircraft came in and got him while we were out on the lake this morning," he said.

"That could be." Stan shaded his eyes with his hand and looked down at the twin Canso still tied to the dock in front of the Hudson Bay Store. Of course, that was it! It had to be! "I don't think Dr. Mulligan's left at all! I think he's still here!"

"And he's going out on that Canso!" Doug cried.

The boys dashed down the slope in the direction of the Hudson Bay Store, but they were not in time. They had not gone more than three or four paces when the pilot shoved the aircraft away from the dock and started the engines.

"They're going!" Del said in dismay. "Now we'll never find out whether he had anything to do with that medicine disappearing!"

"Oh, yes we will!" his brother panted. "We can still stop him. Come on!"

They raced down to the place where the mission boat was pulled up on shore, with Doug leading the way. He started tugging frantically on the boat, in an attempt to shove it into the water. The others saw what he was about to do and joined him, tumbling in as it floated free. By this time, the plane was taxiing up the lake with the wind to get in position for takeoff.

Del jerked the starter rope on the outboard. It started with a high-pitched whine, and the boat began to move forward.

"Are we going to make it?" Doug shouted.

"Sure we will! We've got to!"

The cumbersome aircraft came about slowly and began to inch forward. The boys headed straight for the line of takeoff.

The pilot waved them aside and tried to maneuver to avoid them, but that was useless. He had too much weight to move to get out of the way of the boat.

"What are you going to do now?" Stan asked.

In reply, Del turned the boat straight for the plane.

Ron and Hal Edgren must have been watching them. They came out of Okimaw's house at that point and hurried along the shore to the dock, waving and calling for the boys to come back.

"Come here, Ron!" Doug's voice carried faintly to the shore. "We need you!"

"*Quick!*" Del added, almost screaming to get his voice above the sound of the motors.

They were not sure their voices were heard, but Ron could not mistake their waving gestures. He broke into a run for the nearest boat.

"Come on, Hal!" he called out. "We've got to get out there fast!"

"What's this all about?" Hal asked as he caught up to Ron.

"Search me! But Del and Doug have got some reason for stopping that plane."

"Let's take my boat," Hal said.

By the time the two men reached the aircraft that squatted motionless in the water, the passengers were at the windows.

"I think I see what this is all about now," Ron said quietly to his companion. "I'm going to go over to the plane. OK?"

The field officer nodded.

Dr. Mulligan was on board and came to the cabin door, furiously cursing both Ron and the boys.

"There's no need to get so mad," Mr. Edgren told him coolly. "Let's find out what this is all about."

"Who're you?" Dr. Mulligan demanded.

Del thought he caught a trace of fear in the man's voice.

"I'm the Canadian field officer in charge of this area."

"Then I demand that you get those kids out of our way so we can take off."

"We will, as soon as we find out why they stopped you."

Quickly, Stan and the Davis boys told the field officer what they suspected. Dr. Mulligan glared angrily at them.

"That's a lot of nonsense," he roared.

"Then I suppose you wouldn't mind if we look through your luggage to see whether you do have the roots?" Mr. Edgren asked him.

Dr. Mulligan cursed again. "Nobody's going through my things. I haven't got anything in there to hide, but nobody's going to search me without a warrant."

"Then I think you'd better stay here until the RCMP can come in with a warrant."

"You can't stop me from leaving!" he protested. "You don't have any authority to take me off this plane."

Dr. Mulligan turned to the pilot. "We've fooled around long enough out here. Let's get going!"

At that moment, the pilot took over. "Maybe Hal doesn't have any legal right to take you off this plane, but I do." His voice was cold. "I'm in charge of my aircraft. I can say who flies with me and who doesn't.

You'd better get your gear and get in the boat with them and go back in. Or you can stay here until the RCMP comes in and gives you clearance."

Dr. Mulligan glared at the lanky pilot. "You can't do this to me!"

The pilot laughed dryly. "We'll see about that."

Dr. Mulligan got off the plane and stood in the government man's boat until the pilot got his baggage and lowered it down to him.

"I'll sue you for this!"

"Go right ahead, my friend."

Mr. Edgren moved the cruiser away from the plane so they could hear themselves think.

"There's no need of inconveniencing you. Dr. Mulligan," Ron said, "if you haven't got Oliver Okimaw's roots, you will be free to leave."

"That's right," Mr. Edgren said. "All you've got to do is let me have a look in your gear. If Oliver's heart medicine isn't there, you're free to go."

Dr. Mulligan laughed. "You mean you're going to make me miss my plane because of a few dried up roots?"

"Those 'dried up roots' happen to be very important to Oliver. They're his heart medicine. He's afraid somebody has stolen them."

Dr. Mulligan shook his head as though he could not believe what was happening. "You can't be serious, trying to hold me here for a few roots."

"Have you got them, or haven't you?"

"What would I be doing with them?" he countered.

"You might be planning on selling them to a pharmaceutical house, for one thing – if you felt they really had value as heart medication."

"Believe that old man's junk works? Don't make me laugh."

"Do you have them with you or don't you?" Ron demanded.

The scientist hesitated. "I've got a few roots that I dug myself, but I wouldn't steal any from Okimaw. He's my friend."

"Could we see the roots you have in your gear?" Hal Edgren repeated.

"I guess I can show 'em to you, but it's a lot of nonsense." Reluctantly he dropped to one knee and opened the suitcase. "Here they are. Is that good enough for you?"

Mr. Edgren turned the pieces of dried roots in his hand, thoughtfully. "We'll find out soon."

Dr. Mulligan's belligerence cooled a bit. "You aren't going to take that old savage's word over mine, are you?"

Mr. Edgren's stare was withering. "That 'old savage,' as you call him, is my friend. And I've never known him to tell me anything that wasn't the truth as he saw it."

Dr. Mulligan did not want to go over to the old chief's cabin, but he had no choice. By this time, they were on the dock, and half the men in the village were crowded about, eyeing him silently.

Okimaw studied the roots carefully. There was no doubt in the minds of any of the onlookers in the little cabin that they had located the missing roots.

"Where did you find them?"

The field officer told him.

The chief caught Dr. Mulligan's gaze and said, "You would steal from a friend?" The inflection in his voice was withering.

No answer.

"But why?"

"I think I can answer that for you, Oliver," Mr. Edgren said. "If your heart medicine is really good, a company that makes medicines would probably pay a lot of money for it." He turned to Dr. Mulligan. "Isn't that right?"

The scientist glared at him. "It probably isn't any good, anyway."

Okimaw turned to Mr. Edgren and gestured toward Dr. Mulligan. "Get him out of here!" he rasped. *"I never want to see him again!"*

"You can have him arrested if you want to."

"Get him out of here!" He turned to Dr. Mulligan. "And don't you ever come back to this reserve! Understand?"

"But Okimaw, you don't get it. I'll level with you now. I'm not an anthropologist, and I didn't come here to study the culture of your people. 1 came here to see if you had any herbs or roots that you use for medicine. I work for a pharmaceutical company, and one of my jobs is to find things like your heart medicine. I'll see that you get a lot of money if it is any good."

Okimaw turned that over in his mind. He was uneducated, but he was wise in the ways of men. "You would have stolen the roots from me if you had gotten away from here just now. And you expect me to believe you would be fair with me?" He shook his head. "I will have nothing more to do with you, Mulligan!"

With that, Okimaw turned to Darlene, who had been standing in the corner of the room, watching.

"I must apologize to you." His voice was soft. "You were my friend, after all. My true friend. I am sorry I said you stole from me."

"Don't think anything more about it." Darlene's smile was kind. "I'm only glad you found your roots."

When the Canso was gone with Dr. Mulligan, Hal Edgren and Ron Orlis returned to the old Indian's cabin to talk with him about his medicine.

"No one knows for sure about things like this," the field officer began, "but there *is* a chance that your roots would be worth a lot of money, Oliver. They would have to be tested under laboratory conditions to see the extent that they do affect an ailing heart. If they should prove to be good, I know there will be a drug company who would be very happy to give you a royalty on it. They would share the money they make with you."

"We'll work with you, Oliver," Ron added, "so you can be sure of making contracts with the right people who will protect your interests."

The old Indian took Ron's hand and squeezed it. The look in his eyes revealed the fact that he trusted the youthful missionary.

* * *

During the next few days, Del and Doug worked hard on the addition to the mission house. They framed it and put on the roof and were able to do most of the finishing before the time came for them to go back to Rock Point.

When they had to leave, Stan came down to the aircraft to see them off. "You'll come back, won't you?" he asked.

"We'll sure try."

"I want to thank you again for helping us to get grandfather's medicine back." He paused. "If it had not been for you–."

They were embarrassed by his gratitude and tried to change the subject. "I hope you'll keep on with those Bible studies every week," Doug said.

Stan nodded. "Grandfather and I talked it over. We're both going to study."

"That's great," Del put in.

"He said you have shown him there is something to being a Christian, and he wants to look into it." Then, as though he was afraid the boys would get the wrong impression, he continued quickly. "He doesn't know whether he wants it for himself and neither do I, but we are going to look into it. We are going to have Ron and Darlene teach us."

The boys nodded solemnly. "We'll be praying for you," they said. "We'll be praying for both of you."

THE
DANNY ORLIS
SERIES

The Danny Orlis series, by Bernard Palmer, delivers a blend of adventure, mystery, and suspense through various settings—from the Canadian wilderness to Guatemalan jungles. Danny Orlis, an adept outdoorsman, skilled athlete, and committed Christian, employs his quick thinking, calm bravery, and biblical solutions to confront everyday problems and hair-raising dangers. Early stories focus on Danny navigating school life, sports, and outdoor challenges, while in later books, Danny and his wife Kay provide wisdom and guidance to youngsters facing lifelike situations and challenges. Having sold over two million copies, this series has made Palmer a renowned author in Christian youth literature. Palmer is also the author of the Felicia Cartright series and various other series for Christian youth.

AVAILABLE FROM WWW.ANEKOPRESS.COM